The Red Dress

Dress

Nicholas Hughes

ISBN: 0692813802
ISBN-13: 978-0692813805

DEDICATION

To my mother, who encouraged me to write.

To Kristen, who taught me I could.

Chapter 1

"Dealing with that is not worth a new car."

"I can tell you've never owned a new car."

Some folk collect baseball cards; I collect people. You have a leaky pipe? I know a guy. Want the best deal on three-quarter-inch screws for brick but not drywall? Let me hook you up. Your father disappeared at birth, and now you want to find him? Actually, that's my wife's forte. The point is, I know people and how to connect needs with fixers. Asking the spouse of an old lover for help, however, is not something I'd actively consider.

Which was exactly why Andrea Swope paced before Stephanie Hawthorne's desk this morning. Mind you, she wouldn't get very far. I've always imagined the avenues of Stephanie's mind as a game of baseball. When Andrea arrived an hour late to her appointment, Stephanie assessed the equivalent of the first strike. Actually, that was strike two. Strike one was Andrea's past relationship with me, long dead by the time I married Stephanie. The pacing amounted to strikes three and four. This should say more about Stephanie than my knowledge of baseball.

"I told you already," Andrea said. She was a curvy woman, still attractive despite the onset of years. Unfortunately, that's where my memories came into conflict with the woman who stood before me. A bottle had obviously provided the deep brown of her hair, she wore too much makeup, and no woman, no matter the age, had breasts that perky without artificial help. "I know where Arthur went. He's with that awful Patricia Vice woman. That's no secret."

Stephanie's lips barely moved, yet words crisp and clear filled the room. "I have already explained myself, Mrs. Swope. If you wish, you can either sit down so we can discuss this like adults or continue to pace like a caged dog, in which case you are free to leave."

Andrea looked shocked, sitting without further comment.

"Thank you." Stephanie leaned back. Her sweater, a mix of the colors stolen from a pink poodle and chocolate cake, clashed with the faux black leather of the chair. "As I mentioned before, I don't handle cases involving conflict between spouses. I detest such messes."

Andrea flapped her arms like a spoiled child. "I just want him to stop seeing her. She's using him. I don't want to divorce him." Had my spouse been worth several million dollars, I wouldn't want a divorce either.

"I don't question your intent. However, the damage such information could cause is the issue. I will not be party to the ruination of any person's marriage, warranted or not."

"You have to help," Andrea sputtered. "My friend Michelle Hetter—you remember her—she said you helped her out of a similar bind. She said you'd get results. Expensive results." She said that last bit as if she'd eaten something spoiled.

"Her case was hardly similar." Stephanie rubbed the bridge of her nose with her middle finger. "And what I charge is my affair. People assume that I am the best at what I do. I happen to agree with their assessment. You pay for quality, Mrs. Swope."

Andrea reached forward as if to grab Stephanie's hand. "And I can pay, too. Just help me with Arthur. Imagine the embarrassment for poor Robert." I suspected Robert would survive any such embarrassment, being twenty-five years old and a recent graduate of Harvard. Andrea turned to me for help.

Strike Number Five. Andrea couldn't see it, but I saw the fingers of Stephanie's right hand start to move: thumb to pinky, thumb to ring and forefingers simultaneously, thumb to middle then back again, over and over. It was a miniscule thing, unnoticeable to most, but fidgeting like that meant one of two things. Either Stephanie was lost in thought or she was angry. This didn't require anything close to rumination.

I shrugged and leaned back in my chair. Back when I knew Andrea Swope, then with the surname of Brown, she was the definition of spoiled. After graduating high school, she dated a series of men her father found inappropriate, including a certain rookie private detective. Our relationship was short and turbulent, ending in a spectacular explosion. "Don't look at me," I said. "The last time I changed her mind was to keep from having to brush my teeth every time I ate a pickle."

Andrea's face shifted into well-remembered annoyance, and I felt a spike of pleasure. I had no interest in Andrea's affairs beyond what Stephanie required, and those were based solely on business considerations. So I lounged back, enjoying the moment.

Stephanie's full lips pinched in exasperation. "May I have your attention again, Mrs. Swope?" Andrea's glare failed to faze my wife. "Thank you. I am unable to assist you in this matter. Your cajoling of Mr. Atwell is in vain. Unless you require something else, I have other business to attend to."

Andrea stood up in a huff. "You forget who you're dealing with."

"I assure you, ma'am, I do not."

That only enraged Andrea further. Spittle flew along with her words. "I'll tell everyone about you. How you won't help a woman in need. After I'm done, beggars won't come to you for loose change. I'll ruin you!"

With that, she stomped out of the office, the front door slamming behind her. I walked over to the window and watched as Andrea sped off in a black sedan. Stephanie eyed me as I returned to my seat. "Well, that was fun," I said. "Any other old girlfriends we should dig up?"

"What did you see in that detestable woman?"

"The same thing any guy sees when looking at an attractive woman with a rich father. New car smell."

"You don't see new car smell. Besides, dealing with that is not worth a new car."

"I can tell you've never owned a new car."

Stephanie stood and ran a hand through her hair as she walked around her desk. Any time Stephanie walked anywhere in front of me, I found it hard to think of anything else. My wife was a beauty with curves and soft spots in all the right places. Deep red hair and green eyes belied a sharp mind. Only her God-awful homemade sweaters ruined her looks. "I'll be back."

That broke through my mental block. I raised an

eyebrow. "Where're you going?"

She stopped and eyed me from the doorway. "Any time I deal with one of your former amours, I require some fresh air. Dinner is your responsibility."

The front door slammed as I remained in my chair. "That's the only one you've met." My words echoed pointlessly through empty halls.

Several hours and a large pepperoni pizza later, I sat watching a movie so memorable I have since forgotten the title. I was actually focused on Stephanie, curled up on the couch and reading the same page of her book for the past hour. This was typical whenever she turned down a potentially lucrative job. Stephanie had standards when it came to work. We'd gone in circles about them more than once, but this time I was in full agreement. There was nothing I wanted less than to work for Andrea.

I turned off the television. "I'm going to bed." Stephanie nodded, still pretending to read.

On the way past her seat, I kissed the top of her head. Stephanie put down her book. "Should I have taken the job?"

I laughed despite myself. "God no! Andrea was enough of a pain while we were dating. I have no wish to renew any relationship—professional or private—with that woman."

"But the fee . . ." Stephanie said, waving her hands in the air as if conducting some ethereal orchestra. "It could have been magnificent. Majestic. We could have—"

I knew where this was going. The bill collectors always wanted money. "No fee would be worth dealing with her." Grabbing Stephanie by the wrists, I pulled her to her feet. "Enough of this. Time for bed."

The next day, Stephanie was just as moody as I expected. While I focused on finishing the last few odds and ends on the Buchanan case, Stephanie spent most of her time up in our apartment above the office. Whenever I ran upstairs for one reason or another, she claimed to be cleaning, but her book always sat suspiciously close.

I appreciated her concern for the bank account, but I wouldn't support her melancholy attitude this time around. Stephanie gave me a blank look the first time I brought it up that afternoon. At a second mention, she spouted some drivel about account balances and bills. I shared my disapproval of her argument with an unnecessary zeal. The third time elicited a glare and flip of her head, sending her hair flying in every direction. The mood soon evaporated, and Stephanie returned to her normal self.

Sleep eluded me most of that night. At the break of dawn, I gave up and rolled out of bed, padding off to the kitchen to pour myself a glass of milk, leaving Stephanie undisturbed. I fetched the paper from the front stoop before finding a seat at the kitchen table.

Set in a 32-point font, it filled a prominent place on the front page above the fold. I tapped the article as my eyes focused in on the words.

Society Woman Slain in Robbery

Local socialite Andrea Swope died late last night, apparently murdered in her home. Mrs. Swope was late for a family gathering to celebrate her wedding anniversary when her son, Robert Swope, found the body.

Mrs. Swope was the wife of prominent lawyer Arthur Swope, best known for his successful defense of Andrew Trakenburg.

According to the official police statement, the house was ransacked with several family heirlooms and other valuables reported missing. Current speculation suggests Mrs. Swope startled

the robbers in the middle of their
burglary.

Evidence indicates—

Well, shit.

I stopped reading and looked up. The sound of
footsteps preceded Stephanie into the kitchen. Despite
apparent drowsiness, she caught my mood. Her eyes
narrowed.

"What is it?"

I didn't want to share the news of Andrea's death
so early in the morning, so I mumbled something about
the weather. Stephanie saw through the pretense and
repeated herself. Shrugging, I handed her the paper. The
first read-through took about a minute. Then she started
over, moving slower this time, mouthing the words.

When she reached the end, Stephanie looked up.
"Call James when you get down to the office." I made a
face, but nodded and went to clean up.

Forty-five minutes later, we sat at our desks. I
stared at the phone in disgust while Stephanie shuffled
papers, steadfastly refusing any attempts at conversation.
I'm certain she remained quiet on purpose, in order to
avoid an argument. Andrea's death, while tragic, had
nothing to do with us, and I failed to see the necessity of a

call. Besides, my brother-in-law and I had a mutual dislike for each other. If I could avoid the call, I'd try. James would make it personal. Or I would.

With a sigh and a glare toward my wife, I gave in and dialed, favoring the switchboard over a direct line. A female voice answered on the third ring, and I gave her my name and intended target. I held my peace as a line of people alternately checked on me and placed me on hold. Finally, I recognized the throaty growl in my ear.

I put on an overly jovial tone. "Is that the best way to greet your favorite brother-in-law?"

"Yes. I dislike all of you equally."

"That's unfair." I started ticking off points on my fingers. "First, what did I ever do to you? Second, I want an apology."

"First, you married my sister. Second, no." The last was unequivocal.

Apparently, I wasn't handling it well enough for Stephanie. She motioned for me to pass the call to her. From then on out, my ears only picked up the occasional yes or no. Everything else came to me in hushed tones or mumbled phrases. Arms and legs crossed, I sat back in my chair and eyed my wife as she discussed either Andrea's murder or the birth rate of baby seals.

The conversation soon ended, and Stephanie

turned back to the papers she'd been studying earlier. I continued watching her, anxious for the details. She ignored my attentions. After several minutes with no visible reaction, I cleared my throat. No response. I cleared it again, still eliciting nothing. This pattern continued until Stephanie finally spoke, eyes darting in my direction.

"A glass of water might help. I'd appreciate one as well."

I stood up. We both knew the dance. Upstairs, I filled two coffee mugs with water then returned to the office. Setting a mug in the middle of Stephanie's paperwork, I returned to my desk and watched her in silence. Stephanie moved the mug to a corner of her desk pad with mumbled thanks. A few minutes later, I again cleared my throat.

Her eyes narrowed as the phone rang. I answered it but didn't look away. "Stephanie Hawthorne's office, Daniel Atwell speaking."

The voice on the other end of the phone caught my attention, though my eyes never left Stephanie. It was silky smooth and confident. I pictured it belonging to a woman straight out of a Humphrey Bogart film, all smoking eyes and beautiful calves. "Miss Hawthorne, please."

"She's busy at the moment." Stephanie looked up

and frowned. "Is there something I can help you with?"

"I'm afraid not," the voice cooed. "I must insist that I speak only with Miss—"

"Missus." Best to correct that particular assumption immediately.

"Excuse me?"

"Missus. As in Missus Stephanie Hawthorne. She's married." Stephanie snorted and turned back to her papers. It was a sore point in our marriage.

"Our research said Hawthorne was her maiden name."

"Yep. It sure is."

Our caller uttered some nonsensical noises before falling back to her script. From there, the conversation stalled for several minutes. She insisted on speaking to Stephanie, while I refused to acquiesce to her request.

As I got frustrated, I became more direct. "Listen. This is what's commonly known as a stalemate. Here's the situation. You called me, not the other way around, and I need to know why you want to talk to Mrs. Hawthorne before I pass on the call. If you want to tell me, I'll see what I can do. If not, then I had a wonderful time, but I gotta go."

I received no response as the line went silent but stayed live. A few minutes later, a new voice came on. This time, it was deep, masculine, and carried an air of authority. The Humphrey Bogart to her damsel in distress. "To whom am I speaking?"

"This is Daniel Atwell."

"Mr. Atwell, this is Arthur Swope. I understand you knew my wife, Andrea Swope." I indicated I did with a grunt. "I wish to speak with Stephanie Hawthorne about her death. And you, too, if you are available."

I told him I was free, but I was unsure about the boss. Covering the mouthpiece, I spoke to her. "The city's newest, most eligible widower wants to see if you're free for dinner."

Stephanie grunted and picked up her phone. "This is Stephanie Hawthorne. How may I help you, Mr. Swope?" I cradled my receiver.

Her entire conversation lasted only a minute in total. Nothing beyond a few grunts left Stephanie's lips until she agreed to meet that afternoon. She hung up soon after, spilling the details.

At eleven o'clock, I heard the front door open and footsteps head down the hallway. The man who entered the room stood just under six feet with prematurely grey hair and mustache to match. Tired eyes looked out from beneath bushy brows. Despite this, he stood with a straight back and firm shoulders. He ignored both Stephanie and me as he walked over to the minifridge we kept hidden in a back corner of the office and pulled out a can of Pepsi.

Stephanie gave James Hawthorne, police inspector and my brother-in-law, a dirty look as he collapsed into a chair across from her. "Please, a little decorum."

James grunted in exactly the same way as Stephanie. "Spend all night at a high-profile crime scene with your boss, your boss's boss, the police commissioner, and the mayor all breathing down your neck, and then speak to me of decorum."

"I've endured my own sleepless nights. Manners are something you chose to embrace. You do as you wish. Citing sleep deprivation is nothing more than an excuse."

Growling was another family trait. "So say you."

"Tell me about the murder."

"This one's a doozy. Local socialite killed in her own home in the middle of a botched robbery. All eyes are on me, and the longer I take, the greater my chances of being retired." Nope. I didn't envy him one bit.

"Any leads?" I asked.

James looked at me and rubbed his eyes. "Depends on what you can tell me. As far as the public and the press are concerned, everything is exactly as I said. We told them that some electronics, televisions, and other easily pawned items seem to be missing. Evidence indicates that the theft was in progress when Mrs. Swope came home.

"There were no signs of a break-in, but that's easily explained away. The Swopes kept a key hidden beneath a garden gnome beside their back door. As of this morning, the key is missing. Our chances of finding it are slim to none. We're tracking her movements over the past few days as a matter of routine, but if this was a random act of violence . . ." James shrugged before finishing his drink and setting the empty can on Stephanie's desk.

"Malarkey." Stephanie used a pen to scoot the empty can from her desk to the trash. "Her recent movements would hold little or no significance had this been a random act. Robbery is rarely sufficient cause for murder. Unless supplied with a powerful motivation, most people will balk at crossing that particular line. I understand if you wish to keep certain details private, but do not take me for a ninny.

"You should talk," James said, pointing a finger at Stephanie, "with all the tricks you've pulled over the years."

Stephanie ignored the jab, but returned the glare. "If you truly believed the act random, my call would not warrant a visit from a police inspector."

I often wondered how life would differ had James

or Stephanie chosen different careers. Civility was the exception, not the rule, between the two. Sooner or later, one would reach the point of no return and go off like a tinderbox. It seemed a game between them.

Right then, I had my money on Stephanie. But instead of blowing up, James inhaled with a look of forced calm rolling over his face. It mirrored Stephanie's following her meeting with Andrea. He needed something, and his pride wouldn't let him leave without it. "You're right. There's more we haven't released. The murderer knew her. Someone positioned the body so she looked to be asleep, save for the hole in her chest. It was done respectfully.

"What's odd is that we have the murder weapon, but no bullet. The boys in lab coats found a recently fired revolver beside the body. It was registered to Mrs. Swope, and preliminary ballistics matches the caliber to the wound. More holes line up through the mattress, but there's no sign of the bullet other than where it hit the floorboards. The question is, why take the bullet but leave the gun?" He shifted in his seat.

Stephanie said nothing. James remained calm for as long as he could, but eventually his anger got the better of him. "Say something, will you? Better yet, say something useful. I'm just as smart as you, but you don't see me sitting on top of some imaginary glass tower, lording it over everyone. This thing has me stumped, and I could use some help."

Stephanie raised an eyebrow. "Is that what you want? I refuse to draw conclusions, theories, or assumptions unless I am familiar with the case. You know that." She snapped the last three words. "But I also know you. You didn't come here for assistance, despite your claims. Stop playing games. Spit it out or leave."

That was the tipping point. James leaned over Stephanie's desk. "What I want to know is why Mrs. Swope came here two days ago."

The condescension was too much. Stephanie met her brother's glare, moving only her eyes. "Should you decide to sit and be civil, I'll consider sharing my conversation with Mrs. Swope." With an impassioned cry, James stomped out, only to return seconds later and sit. His desperation was evident as Stephanie started in on Andrea's visit.

Of course, James insisted Stephanie was holding back. I wondered if it was part of his police training or just the paranoid ranting of the only person who knew Stephanie well. Either way, I replayed the events in my head as Stephanie related them. She missed nothing. Which only seemed to make James insist even more vociferously that she was lying.

It did no good. He pried for a good hour before throwing in the towel. I saw him to the door this time. Best practice is to verify that any police officer—family or not—actually leaves; otherwise, you may find an unwelcome surprise. So I watched from the office stoop as he drove off. Stephanie told me to shut up when I commended her on a job well done. I complied.

Our conversation with Arthur Swope that afternoon was just as productive. My standing practice is to research any prospective client before we meet. Since Stephanie failed to indicate otherwise, I proceeded to do so.

Arthur Swope proved to be a prominent lawyer. Considered the black sheep of his family, he attended Harvard in a traditionally Yale-educated family. He worked as a small-time lawyer at a prestigious firm for seven years before starting his own firm with classmate Julian Stout. Soon, Swope & Stout became one of the premier criminal law firms, reaching moderate fame for successfully defending high-profile clients in criminal court. Swope met and married Andrea four months after the well-publicized trial of Edward Trakenburg. Robert, his only child, followed a few months later. Stout died two years ago, leaving Swope the sole senior partner of the multimillion-dollar firm. Rumor had Robert making partner soon, but nothing formal had happened yet.

By the time I finished, Swope was due. Routine dictated I greet any known guest in the waiting room at the front of the building. I left the office a few minutes before four and took my normal position for such occasions—an old armchair at odds with the room's décor.

Over an hour later, I stood with a sigh. Stephanie insisted that business hours end promptly at five. Unexcused tardiness put Swope on rocky ground. Yet, as I prepared to close up shop, the front door opened, and a blast of cold air ushered in a well-dressed man. Arthur Swope looked closer to forty-two than the sixty-five years he wore. His face was red—from the cold, perhaps—but I doubted that precise shade ever went away. Ignoring my greeting as well as the coat rack, he threw a grey wool overcoat over a nearby chair and started down the hall.

"Mr. Arthur Swope," I said, entering the office seconds after our guest. Stephanie scowled at our interruption as she put down her latest cheap romance novel. Swope took a seat in the chair farthest from my desk.

Stephanie cleared her throat. "I am sorry for your loss."

"Thank you." The tone was the same he'd used on

the phone.

"How may I help you, Mr. Swope?"

"This is private. Send your man home."

Stephanie nodded. "Mr. Atwell, go home."

"Done." I didn't bother to hide my insolence.
"Honey, I'm home."

Stephanie snorted. "There. Satisfied?"

"No. He hasn't moved."

"We both live here, Mr. Swope. He has every right
to be in this room. More so than you. Besides, if I sent Mr.
Atwell away, I would only be obligated to inform him of
any pertinent details. I have few secrets from my husband.
Secrets make for an uncomfortable marriage bed, and I
like my rest. This saves us time. You may trust his
discretion as much as you trust mine."

For a moment, I thought Swope would leave. The
prospect failed to bother me. I disliked being informed I
lacked professionalism. Good riddance.

A moment later Swope nodded. "I'm not sure I
can trust your discretion, but as I see it, I have little choice.
I want information, and I'm willing to pay for it." He
pulled out a bundle of bills from a pocket of his suit coat.
They were well-worn and bound with rubber bands.
Swope placed them on Stephanie's desk. "Andrea visited
you yesterday. I want to know why."

Stephanie grimaced. "I expected this. Under normal conditions, I keep any communication between myself and clients as confidential as possible within the limits of the law. I see no reason to change that inclination, despite your loss."

"My wife was murdered. The least you can do is help."

"I have. The police have already discussed Mrs. Swope's visit with me. My part in this matter is finished."

Anger smoldered in Swope's eyes. "Hardly. I can already tell I don't like you, Mrs. Hawthorne, but from what I hear, you are the best. Andrea wanted to hire you. Well, so do I."

"No. You're in grief, Mr. Swope, and not thinking rationally. Your wife's body is not yet in the ground. The police have just started their investigation. To interfere now would prove a folly on both our parts. Give the police time. They are quite competent in these matters."

"They'll screw it up. They're good at that, too. I want you to look after my interests here. Find out who killed my Andrea."

And so it went. Swope tried different methods to convince Stephanie, including pulling out another stack of bills, dressed the same as the first. I saw Stephanie's hand twitch at the sight. Swope must have missed it; otherwise, he might have repeated that trick again.

Eventually, I got bored. I sighed as I looked at my watch: a quarter past six. Four eyes turned toward me, effectively ending the meeting. Swope gathered his money and left the office without another word. Stephanie jerked her head at the door, and I followed Swope out. He'd already donned his coat when I reached the front room. I crossed the room and opened the door for him. Half across the sill, cold air swirling about the two of us, Swope stopped and looked at me. "You were lucky to know her." Then he was gone.

I locked the door behind him and returned to the office. Stephanie met me at the doorway. "We'll send flowers. Nothing too extravagant, however—she was your *former* girlfriend. I don't like the idea of someone believing you still harbored feelings for her." She headed upstairs to start dinner, while I closed down the office for the night.

Chapter 2

"That another romance? They had sex yet?"

We wrote off the Andrea Swope affair after Arthur Swope's departure that winter. Of course, that was only professionally. We sent flowers, and I attended the funeral later that week. Stephanie had halfheartedly offered to join me, but I refused, wanting privacy. I appreciated the offer.

As winter turned to spring and spring into summer, a slew of mundane cases crossed our path. Such were our bread and butter—cases solved in a day or two that paid well for the time involved. Only one case included a hefty fee and an intense three days. Everything else involved searching for missing people—including an elderly man trying to enlist for World War II—locating vehicles misplaced by drunks, and finding a lost dog for a local girl. The dog was pro bono.

I followed any developments on Andrea's murder out of personal interest. That first week, newspapers printed fresh leads and theories every day, mixing new information with the old. Slowly, it changed. Front page stories fell below the fold and were soon mixed into the clutter of the inner pages before drying up altogether. By June, any commentary on Andrea's murder was rare.

That wasn't to say we heard nothing. More than once, James stomped into our office in a whirlwind of accusations and bad temper. He continued to drop tidbits here and there when visiting us on other matters. I barely noticed these tirades, long since coming to the conclusion that Andrea's murder wouldn't be solved.

That all changed on a Tuesday in early July. Stephanie and I had wrapped up our last case the week before and had nothing new coming down the pipeline. For a business that relied on constant turnover, the lack was disconcerting. I was trying not to worry about it, instead catching up on a few odds and ends I'd been putting off. The phone's chime startled me, and I let two or three rings slip by before I answered it. "Stephanie Hawthorne's office, Daniel Atwell speaking."

I recognized the voice on the other end of the line. Arthur Swope was politer than the last time we spoke, but not by much. "Mr. Atwell, I want to see Mrs. Hawthorne this afternoon." It didn't take a valedictorian to figure out what he wanted, but this time I paused before rejecting him. Stephanie had been more pompous than usual lately and could use her bubble burst. I set the appointment for three that afternoon. We parted ways, and I went to tell the resident genius.

Stephanie reacted as I expected, growling and complaining. I ignored it, knowing full well she coddled an allergy to work. She knew I wasn't listening and shut up. An Internet search and a few phone calls dredged up little in the way of new information on Arthur Swope. Only two items seemed worth mentioning.

One: Since the death of his wife, Arthur Swope had thrown himself into his work. The firm had flourished, taking on and winning only high-profile cases. I found Robert Swope's distance from these cases interesting, but wrote it off as a combination of family and office politics.

Two: For the first time since Julian Stout's death, Arthur Swope was searching for a new partner in the firm. Several names populated the rumored list of potential candidates, which included Robert only as a long shot with no explanation as to why.

Compiling everything took about an hour and filled all of half a page. I proceeded to add a second dated copy to our files and handed the finished work to Stephanie. She read it before returning to her latest bodice-ripper.

I gave her a minute of silence before speaking up. "Instructions?"

She looked up from her book. "For now, nothing." I opened my mouth in rebuttal, but she cut me off. "However, I have letterhead in the printer. I suspect this meeting will be folly, but perhaps it might be useful. Following that, shut up."

I prepared the letterhead as she requested and found myself with nothing more to do. Nothing about waiting excited me, and silence was never my strong suit. That left entertaining myself.

"Glad to see you're all relaxed," I said, leaning back in my chair. Stephanie grunted, but I plowed through the onslaught. "That another romance? They had sex yet?"

A grunt.

"Really? That's surprising. I thought sex was standard operating procedure for those types of novels. You're at least sixty pages in. There's got to be some law against it."

Another grunt.

I got up and walked across the room to one of the bookcases set into the wall. Selecting the eighth volume from a set of secondhand law books, I opened it at random. "Double jeopardy, double indemnity, double trouble, Double Dragon, St. George and the Dragon, Puff the Magic . . . Maybe I should look under *R*." I selected another volume from the shelf.

"Shut up." Stephanie's voice filled the room. "You wish to goad me into action, but I ask you what action should I take? I see nothing reasonable. Mr. Swope will either be here or not. No amount of goading will change that salient fact. Now will you sit? You look like a terrier hunting gazelle on the African savanna."

Halfway back to my seat, the front door opened, and I detoured around to the hall. Swope stood in the waiting room, looking much the same as before, but now a melancholy air seemed to have settled about him. I guided him down the hallway and into the same chair before Stephanie's desk.

Stephanie carefully marked her spot before setting her book on the far corner of her desk. "Mr. Swope. How may I help you?"

He waved his hand like the question was a fly in need of shooing. Apparently, the brashness was also permanent. "I've taken a special interest in you since my wife's death. God knows why, but I have. You're a very interesting person, Ms. Hawthorne. But I do have one question. When I came here last winter, you refused my commission. Why?"

Stephanie adjusted herself in her chair before

speaking. "As I told you before, I'm not in the habit of explaining myself, Mr. Swope. I'll make an exception this time; there won't be a second. When you arrived, your wife had just died. You were grieving. Grief, while natural, prohibits clear thinking. You were at a mental disadvantage. To accept your charge felt akin to theft, and I like to earn my fee.

"Also, consider the police. They are men and women specially trained to track, apprehend, and convict those guilty of societal transgressions. You refused them time to do their jobs. My interference would have only stirred up already murky water. Besides, my brother is the police detective in charge of your case. One must stand with family on occasion; otherwise, we lose ourselves in chaos."

Swope stirred, setting his jaw. "That's all fine and good, but they've found nothing. They're washed up. It's time for someone else to try. I want it to be you. If you're half as good as I hear, you'll solve it by the end of the week."

Stephanie smirked. "Hardly. The case is cold. This endeavor will be costly—to you in money and me in time. Any new leads would prove laborious to discover and follow. I doubt that I could achieve your goal within such time constraints and would refuse if so constricted."

"It isn't fair that the police arrest countless junkies and adrenaline addicts on worthless charges, only to leave Andrea's death unsolved. I want you to find Andrea's killer."

"You wax poetic, Mr. Swope. I am certainly willing to try; otherwise, we would not be speaking. Your purpose in visiting was readily apparent, and the police have had enough time to do their job. Family ties only go so far. But you need to know what you are facing. Let me be frank. This will not be cheap. You will get what you pay for, but at what I deem a fair rate. Nor will my fee be contingent upon success. I—not you—will decide when all avenues are exhausted and the investigation is over. At that point, I will present my bill."

"Cost doesn't matter. I won't give up."

Stephanie smiled at Swope's comment, thin lipped but genuine. "All I request is for you to be prepared for the long haul. Satisfactory?" Swope nodded. "Good. Mr. Atwell will draw up the required documents and present them for your signature tomorrow. Now. I have questions. Most of what I know about the case comes from easily accessible public sources, but you were much better acquainted with your wife and her habits. Do you know why someone would want her dead?"

Swope looked startled. "Why? The police already

asked me that. Don't you have something new?"

Stephanie sighed. "I am not the police and lack the information they've already gathered. All investigations are built on the same core questions. Should I lack that information, then the investigation will be flawed at a fundamental level. Do I need to repeat the question?"

He shook his head. "No. I can't think of anyone who'd want Andrea dead. She was a lovely woman. Everyone loved her."

"Did your wife have any enemies?"

"Didn't I just answer that question?"

"The papers claimed that your wife was a well-known activist," Stephanie said. "Which organizations did she frequent?"

"Andrea worked with plenty of groups—everything from animal rights to school reform. I couldn't name all of them, even before she died. All I remember is the night before her death, she talked about some charity called MBE." He pronounced each letter separately.

"Stands for Mother's for Better Education," Swope continued. "They were some upstarts who tried to force school reform in the local districts. I believe they disbanded a few months ago from lack of support."

Stephanie grunted. "A shame. Any other organizations?"

"That I can think of? Just the animal shelter down on Fifth and Main. That was an on-and-off affair for years. It became predictable and routine. We all knew when she would leave and return like a bad cold."

"I understand there was to be a celebration of your anniversary the night she died. Who was invited?"

Swope shook his head. "Just some close friends and family. I'll vouch for each of them."

"Even so, I'll need a list of names, though I doubt I'll learn something the police haven't. Unless I hire some competent help, I have just Mr. Atwell and myself, while they have an army of trained men at their disposal. This party was obviously not at your home. Where was it held?"

"We had rented the ballroom down at Anthony's for the night."

"Why not at your house? Surely you had enough space."

Swope ran a hand through his hair. "Take your pick. Vanity. We had no urge to clean up afterward. Those and other aspects made it simpler to have someone else handle the risks."

Stephanie grunted. "What risks?"

"Some of the invitees can be excitable, especially when alcohol is tossed into the mix. Repairs were never part of the dinner plans. Also," Swope paused and his tongue poked out from between his lips before he went on, "certain people—especially my daughter-in-law—enjoy the hobby of borrowing items while forgetting to ask permission."

I cut in. "They stole."

Swope had apparently forgotten about me and now glared in my direction before returning a sullen gaze to Stephanie. "We often had to request the return of those items. To add insult to injury, they were usually ruined. This way we hoped to avoid any potential problems."

"You mention your daughter-in-law. Why?"

"There was nothing specific, just suspicions. Helen—that's her name— would come over, and one thing or another would go missing. She has expensive tastes. I don't know how Robert satisfies them on his income." Swope leaned back in his chair and crossed his arms.

Stephanie did the same, unconsciously mimicking him. "One would expect the son of the senior partner to garner a more lucrative salary."

Swope's face tightened up. "Pay for young lawyers is low because they have yet to prove themselves. I lived on canned vegetables and packaged pasta at his age and was still more successful than he is. Robert has to earn his salary; I won't give that boy a damn thing until he earns it."

"Why did Robert find the body rather than you? I would have expected you to be at home as well."

"I knew I'd be stuck at the office that night until just before the party. I brought my clothes with me, changed into them there, and headed over to Anthony's. Before you ask, I was alone." He took a deep breath. "But because of my obligations, Robert agreed to drive Andrea to the party. He was devoted to her. They were always close and . . ." Swope looked at his watch. "Damn, I'm late." The elder lawyer jumped to his feet and moved toward the door. "Call me at the office should you need anything."

Stephanie said something then, but neither Swope nor I caught it until she repeated herself. Swope stopped in his tracks.

"First, I want a retainer," Stephanie said. "Five thousand dollars. Daniel can collect it tomorrow when he brings the paperwork by for you to sign. Second, I want to see the room where your wife died. Has it changed?"

"No," Swope said. "I sleep in one of the guest rooms. Andrea haunts our bedroom. At least her memory does. The police hauled part of the bed away, but the rest of it's the same. You're welcome to it."

Stephanie nodded, and I saw Swope out before returning to my desk. "Well, I suppose we should change tonight's plans now that we have a case. Which should we skip, the movie or the fancy restaurant?" Perhaps both, if my luck was in.

"Nonsense." Stephanie stood. "This case lacked any significant development since Mrs. Swope's death. One more night won't change a thing. Besides, I've looked forward to tonight for two weeks." Of course she had.

She paused at the door. "Do you believe his naivety? Everyone loved his wife. Rubbish. No one is universally loved. Besides, I experienced that dubious pleasure myself and still do not see what he—or you—saw in her."

"Breasts. Don't go making faces. That makes up for a lot when youth and inexperience mistake lust for love. I understand something of the difference now."

Stephanie raised an eyebrow. "Don't be an ass."

I got my legs under me and joined Stephanie at the door. "Unless you rather I lust after your body, rather than love the—"

The words ceased as pain blossomed in my arm. I rubbed where Stephanie hit me as she unclenched her fist. Fifteen minutes later, we had changed and were out the door.

The film was passable, at best.

Chapter 3

"Would anyone wish to harm Mrs. Swope?"

"Don't call her that. To me, she'll always be Mom, but you . . . She deserves better."

I found myself at the Swope Law Office at ten the next morning. It took up every floor of an old six-story converted storefront. While the brick exterior matched something from the 1930s, extensive remodeling inside had created a modern atmosphere. A mellow burnt-orange covered the walls, with only the odd potted plant and mass-produced landscape left to break the monotony. A reception desk occupied the center of the room and was manned by a blond in professional attire. Couches and chairs, more comfortable-looking than they probably were, lined the walls, along with the requisite three-month-old magazines fanned out on tables around the room.

I approached the most attractive thing in the room, returning her cold eye with patented smile number two. "Daniel Atwell to see Arthur Swope."

She spoke in a clipped manner, making no attempt

to hide her distaste. "Mr. Swope doesn't argue cases anymore. You can meet with another lawyer. Perhaps Ms. Salsburg." She picked up her phone and dialed.

I reached out and depressed the switch hook. She looked angry, so I switched to smile number four. "That's okay. I'll find my way. He's expecting me."

"I'm sorry, Mr. Hawthorne, but I'm afraid not." I didn't rise to the occasion. Mama would've been proud. "No one is allowed into the offices unescorted. Client confidentially. You'll just have to wait until I'm free to see you up."

"Okay." I slouched forward, elbows on the reception desk, the model of patient insolence.

She pointed to one of the chairs against the wall. "You can have a seat over there."

"I know," I said, looking up at her and switching back to smile number two.

Her lips pinched. It only made her cuter. "Follow me."

"No need for that, Heather." The mousy speech sounded from behind me, and I turned to see exactly the type of man you would expect to own such a voice. "I'll take him up to Father's office. I need to drop off the Varner case." The receptionist nodded, short and quick, clearly happy to be rid of me.

My guide lacked any sort of chin and had ears too large for his head. I sampled his handshake—much too limp—as we paused before the elevator. "Robert Swope. We'll have to stop at my office for that file I mentioned before I take you up." He paused as we entered and started the assent. "I understand my father hired you to investigate Mom's death?"

I agreed, but corrected him on who was hired. Robert nodded and continued on unruffled. "Whatever he told you about Mom, I'm sure he got it wrong."

That was an interesting statement. I made to address it, but before I could, the doors opened and he stepped out into a carpeted hallway. It looked much like the lobby, but sterile. Some of the doors, each marked with a plaque, sat open, but most were shut. Robert led me down two halls before stopping at a door marked with his name and title. We entered a room just large enough for its contents, painted red and lined with overflowing bookcases. Two overstuffed chairs sat before a well-worn wooden desk. "What do you mean your father got it wrong?" I made myself comfortable in the chair closest to his desk.

His answer was punctuated by the ruffling of papers and the opening of drawers. "In my father's mind, Mom was perfect. He never saw any of her flaws. I did.

Everyone else did. But not the great lawyer. It didn't matter how many times she insulted him in public; she never blemished."

"How did you feel about her?"

Robert paused, looking at me over a sheet of paper. "She was my mother. How do you think I felt about her? I loved her. I don't know how many times I've gone to call her since her death, only to realize she can't answer. And every time I do, I remember, and the wounds open back up."

"Would anyone wish to harm Mrs. Swope?"

"Don't call her that," he rasped. "You knew her yourself. To me, she'll always be Mom, but you . . . She deserves better."

I shrugged. "Your mother's and my time together ended long ago. This profession requires me to keep emotions distant; otherwise, it compromises objectivity and results. It may sting, but it's all I have. Do you understand?"

He dropped his head and went back to the drawers. "She didn't have any friends—none that I can think of, at least—but no one wanted her dead."

"I take it she was only close to your father?"

"When I was growing up, she talked about a few friends, but I never met any of them. I thought they were imaginary. Gradually she stopped talking about them. But even with Father, she was often distant. The only person she seemed to have any emotional connection with was Helen, and only regarding that animal shelter."

"That seems like a lonely life."

"I agree. But Mom didn't mind. She reveled in it. Maybe those charities made up for it somehow, provided a place to focus the attentions she gave no one else."

"What about the two of you?"

Robert shook his head as he shuffled through another stack of papers. "We were close, but over the last few years things got strained. We were too alike to have a harmonious relationship. We made due." His smile was bittersweet. "I wish we hadn't argued as much now, but hindsight and all that."

"What can you tell me about these charities she worked with?" I asked. "I need a list of them if possible."

He paused and then giggled. I want to be fair, but the man giggled. "'Worked with' might be too strong a phrase. Mom was a great starter but never much more. She breezed into a place, declaring their cause her own, and then promptly changed everything. Didn't make her many friends. If anyone balked, Mom would throw money around until she got her way. Then she'd grow bored and quit." Robert shook his head. "I can get you a list before you leave."

He paused before going on. "I think they only kept her around because she was a monetary godsend. Each received tons of donations thanks to her connections. She rarely involved herself with the same charity more than once, so if a group got the opportunity, they seized it."

"What about the MBE?"

He shook his head. "I doubt it. That was her pet cause when she died, but she'd only been with them for about a week. They had yet to fully experience the brunt of her attentions. Any hatred had yet to climax. The only organization she worked with consistently was the animal shelter. Unlike the others, she never tried to reorganize it. She even brought home an abandoned kitten a month before her death."

"I understand you found your mother's body."

Robert paused for a long minute before speaking, physically gathering himself to continue. "Yes. Mom and I had talked earlier that day. She was having second thoughts about the anniversary party. At the time, my parents' marriage was under a lot of stress, and she didn't feel a giant gala would help. But Father insisted and she went along. That night wasn't even around their anniversary. I don't know who missed that detail, but it reeks of Father.

"Anyway, Mom wanted to cancel the entire thing. I thought it was cold feet or embarrassment or something stupid, so I convinced her to leave it be. I went to the house because I'd promised to drive her. It was the only way I could get her to attend. But I was late." Tears formed at the corner of his eyes, and he paused to wipe them away.

I jumped into the silence. "Put a pin in that. What's the relationship between your father and Patricia Vice?"

Robert took his time gathering himself and sat back in his chair with his eyes closed. He remained that way as he spoke. "Years ago, Patricia Vice was an organizer at one of the charities Mom helped with. That's where Father met her. Her husband died just after her election to Congress. She and Father kept in touch, and now that she's running for another term, she enlisted my father's help as an advisor. Beyond that, nothing."

He opened his eyes and attempted a weak smile before starting in again at the pile before him. Near the bottom, he pulled out a manila folder. "Found it. You are quite a distraction, Mr. Hawthorne." I let it slide. "Now we can head to Father's office."

Instead of standing right away, I sat there

watching him. The abrupt ending felt contrived and rubbed me the wrong way. I had more questions, along with sowing Stephanie's seeds, and yearned to continue prying. But then the moment passed. It would keep for now.

The trip up to Arthur Swope's office took only a few minutes. When the elevator doors opened, we stood on the top floor in a bare, white hallway with two doors, one on either side. Using the door on the left, we entered into a spacious office painted dark green. Bookshelves lined the walls, filled with books and binders of the same size if not the same color. Even a bust of Socrates stood against the wall. Arthur Swope sat behind a massive wooden desk, his back to a floor-to-ceiling plate glass window which looked out onto the street below.

Swope never looked up as we approached. While I produced the documents that needed to be signed, Robert held out the folder to his father. I thought it impossible for Robert to become any less intimidating, but he succeeded. "Here's the Varner files you wanted. Also, I brought that detective you hired." A thumb shot out at me.

The senior Swope scowled at his son. "I can see that. What took you so long? Miss Swanson informed me of his arrival half an hour ago."

Robert mumbled something unintelligible and all but ran from the room. I looked back to Swope as the folder hit his desk. "Bad timing?"

Arthur's eyes locked onto mine. The look soon softened, but in the same way one compares the firmness of stone. "Is that the paperwork you need me to sign?" He pointed at the papers in my hand.

Nodding, I passed him the paperwork. He glanced through it and signed at the bottom. The retainer came next. I had to ask for it, but he picked up his phone without a word, punched in three digits, and asked Miss Swanson to bring up the check. We sat in silence while we waited. I had only one other question to ask, but I kept my trap shut. Swope obviously saw me as an inconvenience more than anything else, so I kept my peace as he returned to his paperwork. Ten minutes later, the door opened and the blond receptionist from downstairs entered. She glared at me as she delivered an envelope to Swope. Obviously, she had an issue with me, but I'll admit that I enjoyed her departure for multiple reasons.

Swope handed me the envelope. Inside I found both a check and a list of charities. Either they'd had it ready or Robert worked fast. "Will that be all, Mr. Atwell?" There was one more request, and I stated it as directly as possible

"A key?" Swope harrumphed. He reached into the center desk drawer and withdrew a set of keys, selected one, and handed it over. "Use this. I keep it around the office in case of emergencies or if I need to send for something. Just lock up when you're done."

"You send your receptionist on personal errands?"

"Don't act so startled. You do the same for Ms. Hawthorne yourself. But no, Miss Swanson is my personal secretary. She's just filling in downstairs today. Temporary duty. Now if you are done questioning how I run my firm, I have business to attend to." I skedaddled.

I summoned the elevator and rode it down. The main lobby looked much the same as when I left, save for two new additions. A gentleman in his midfifties occupied a seat in a corner reading last month's *Newsweek*. Also, a handsome brunette of indeterminate age stood with Miss Swanson. I enjoyed the view for a minute. It reminded me of looking at two different flowers in full bloom, each beautiful in its own way. You can state a preference, but are unable to explain why.

The brunette noticed me first. Something about her face struck a chord in my head, but I couldn't pin it down. Swanson turned and, seeing me, approached. Her eyes bore through my skull. I was glad looks couldn't actually kill.

She stopped less than a foot away. "I don't like what you're doing." Her words hissed through the air. Crossed arms below her breasts only accentuated her displeasure. And my distraction.

I tried to look nonchalant. "Sorry. If you want to fill out a comment card, perhaps I can send it in for repair."

Sighing, one hand rose to pinch the bridge of her nose. "Taking advantage of Mr. Swope. He's a good man, even if his wife wasn't. I want you to drop this and let the police handle it. He shouldn't have to pay you for the same work. What can you do that they can't?"

Rhetorical question, but I was waiting for such an opening. "Civil servants are bound by certain laws and restrictions. Private detectives have their own, but different. That makes things a bit more interesting.

"Also consider this: Mrs. Hawthorne is a genius with a taste for too much money. But we can also use that wealth to test theories and suppositions that the police can't afford. Take that missing bullet from Mrs. Swope's murder. If the police find it, they can match it to the gun but not much else. We have more options. For example, any fingerprint oil on a bullet is destroyed when the bullet is fired." I made a gun with my hand, shaping the pointer and middle fingers as the barrel and my thumb as the hammer.

"Some experimental labs have found microscopic etchings in the metal from the oils in your fingers. This allows them to pull a fingerprint from those impressions. It's all very high-tech and complicated. I don't understand it all. What I do know is that it's kind of cool, very useful, and even more expensive." I dropped my hand back to my side. The rest was up to her.

Swanson's face had darkened as I waxed on, and now it was a storm cloud. "Get out." I flashed smile number three as I stepped around her and out the front doors.

Chapter 4

"Don't give me that. You can focus on dresses and shoes; I'll stick with the blood."

The weather outside the Swope offices was more than a little enjoyable. The kind perfect for walking. Unfortunately, Stephanie had set a curfew, and I suspected it was closing in. A glance at my watch told me I was correct. Traffic was light and I made it home in time, but I did drive a bit slower than usual.

The office sat empty when I returned. I had expected to find Stephanie at her desk, but her absence left me a bit dumbfounded. If the day was as busy as she claimed, she should be at her desk, not gallivanting around somewhere. I went in search of my wife.

The meeting and storage rooms downstairs were empty, as were our living quarters upstairs. My only clue to her disappearance lay in the coffee pot. It had still been hot when I left that morning, but now all semblance of heat had fled. I went back downstairs and into the garage. Stephanie's nondescript silver Ford was absent from its usual spot.

There was nothing to do but wait. A stack of bills and bits of miscellaneous paperwork helped pass the time. Half an hour later, I finished what tasks remained; still no sign of Stephanie. This seemed more than enough reason for aggravation. Remember my curfew and understand the frustration.

I took the stairs two at a time. Stephanie wanted me home by a certain time, yet she was nowhere to be found. The selfishness galled me, especially considering that she would never consider it selfish. I flopped on the couch and turned the television on to a summary of last night's game. The Tigers had lost by a significant margin, and I wanted to know why.

Even so, I could barely sit through the overview. When the anchors moved on, I grabbed my hat and keys, shooting downstairs and into the garage. The garage door opened just as I jumped into my dark-green Jeep, which had passed its prime last century. I waited until Stephanie pulled in before stepping back out to stand by her passenger door.

Stephanie was already out of the car, two bags in hand, before I could open my mouth.

"Ready to go?" The question came nonchalantly from over her shoulder as she headed inside, leaving both car and house doors open. I kept silent. She reemerged a moment later, minus her shopping. "Well?"

I pursed my lips but climbed in the Ford. "Swope gave me his personal spare key. We can keep it as long as we need, but he's going to want it back." That kicked off my report on the morning's activities. Once I finished, Stephanie asked a few questions, to which I had mostly cursory answers. It only took about fifteen minutes more before Stephanie pulled into the driveway of a house on the outskirts of town.

As we walked up to the door, two thoughts occurred to me. First, I wondered how she knew where the Swope's lived. It wasn't exactly common knowledge. Then the second question popped in. Who really needed a house that enormous? Not that I would refuse one. The question was more of a rhetorical one, but I swear I heard our knock echo as we waited out front before trying the key.

The whole house was the perfect model of opulence. Tiles of a rich black-and-white mosaic covered the entryway, while hardwood floors filled the rest of the house. An ornamental chandelier hung from the ceiling, and the walls were a spotless white. On our left, a staircase lined with thick tapestries led to the upper floors. Who had tapestries anymore? To our right sat a dining room filled with china and crystal which looked like it belonged in the

Russian Imperial Palace, while a kitchen could just be seen down the hall. I was almost afraid to see what it held. Artwork, probably more expensive than it looked, hung on crimson walls between the tapestries.

Stephanie headed into the dining room. She said nothing, instead just absorbed the atmosphere. It was a spacious room with unadorned white walls. A tiered chandelier hung above the fine mahogany table that cost more than I made in a year which sat in the middle of the room. Nothing piqued my interest, so we soon moved on to the kitchen.

There we ran across Mrs. Swope's adopted cat. She was covered in mottled grey-and-brown fur and obviously still a kitten. Her green eyes followed us from her throne on the windowsill. Stephanie stopped to pet her and refilled her empty water dish from the kitchen faucet. The cat deigned to accept the attention—at least until I went to pet her. I shrugged as she darted from the room.

The rest of the house came from the same overly opulent mold. From time to time, Stephanie stopped and focused on one item or another, seemingly more out of idle curiosity than anything else. Who finds it surprising that books on law, politics, and history fill the shelves in a lawyer's library? Other rooms were filled with everyday riffraff. We meandered up one flight of stairs, then a second, until we reached our destination.

Stephanie mumbled something as we stood in the doorway of the master bedroom.

I leaned forward and whispered in her ear. The room seemed to demand a certain amount of solemnity. "Repeat that?"

"Stay here." With that, she entered the room. A light layer of dust covered everything, marking Stephanie's path with clear footprints. The dresser looked suspiciously bare, despite the few items on it. Other aspects looked quite typical, such as the closed closet and the two side tables. Only the bed with its missing mattress—and accompanying bloodstain—failed to appear normal.

Stephanie worked her way around the room, remaining intently focused on specific areas. The dresser and its contents were the first to receive her ministrations. After riffling through the contents of the drawers, she pulled a handful of baubles from the jewelry box which sat atop the dresser and examined them before stuffing them away again. Andrea's closet held more interest as she picked though the dresses. Again, three or four dresses were pulled out and then put away. When Stephanie finished that, she grabbed a nearby chair in order to search the boxes stacked at the top of the closet. That was the fastest search yet. Next came the floor of the closet. A pair of red heels—worn down to a more sedate "hold me" rather than their original "fuck me" vibe—soon sat next to her on the floor. Stephanie stood and handed the shoes to me.

Finally, she turned her attention to the bed frame. It was wide, probably a king, with four wooden posts jutting upward. A bloodstain the size of a dessert plate, marked the center of the floor underneath the bed frame, and Stephanie stepped between the slats to kneel beside it. She rubbed her hands over the floor in different places, slowly narrowing her focus to the indentation the bullet had made when it hit the floor. At first she used only her fingertips to examine it, but soon enough she had her nose pressed against the floor, moving about to examine the pockmark from different angles. Half an hour passed before she stood and returned to the doorway.

"Your turn."

I raised an eyebrow. "I'm released then?" She nodded, ignoring my tone, and I handed her back the heels.

My examination took less time than hers, but don't quote me on that. I ended up focusing on all the same areas Stephanie had, including the jewelry box and closet, with little to show for it. Each piece of jewelry gleamed, but it was not of the best quality. It took me a minute to realize that all of it was paste. The dresser also held nothing of interest, nor did the bedside tables. Hoping to avoid a goose egg, I turned my attention to the bed and the stain.

The bed held little if any interest beyond a few indentations and scratches on the posts where the mattress would have rubbed against the wood. That suggested a habit I had no wish to confirm. Simply put, the bloodstain was the most interesting thing in the room. I knelt in the same spot as Stephanie had and examined it. It took a minute to notice the incongruity. From the doorway, the floor seemed indented, but now I could see a chunk missing. Rubbing the spot with my fingers, I felt a tiny slope on one edge where the bullet hit, but the other side was jagged and torn.

I looked up at Stephanie. "The bullet didn't ricochet, it impacted. Someone dug it out."

Her lips turned up in a brief acknowledgement. "No matter what James said, I suspect he knows the truth. Forensics doesn't often miss such things."

I got up and returned to the doorway. "I expected more blood."

Stephanie glanced at me, frank disapproval in her eyes. I went on. "Don't give me that. You can focus on dresses and shoes; I'll stick with the blood."

She said nothing as we returned downstairs. At the front door, I pointed to the heels she still held in her hand. "You plan on taking them with you? It's not your best color."

Sighing, she slipped them beneath a table beside the door. "Call Mr. Swope and ask for permission to remove these from the house." Then she was out the door.

I doubted her apparent casualness. It rang false and my gut agreed. When she'd handed the stilettos to me, nothing seemed the least bit abnormal about them. As I shut the door, I took another look. They were worn, but they were still in good condition. But just as I was sure Stephanie was more intrigued by them than she let on, I felt positive I was missing something.

We sat in silence for a minute. Sun streamed through the car windows, causing an instant sheen of sweat to appear on my skin. There seemed to be nothing to say, and I wondered what Stephanie was thinking.

She broke the silence first. "I wanted to send you after Patricia Vice alone. Unfortunately, I think I'll need to see her myself." My wife turned the key in the ignition, and the car came to life.

"I've always wanted to meet a politician," I said as I reclined my seat and propped my hat over my eyes for a nap. "Rumor says they smell like licorice."

"You don't even like licorice."

"I feel the same way about politicians."

Chapter 5

"What do you mean 'feeling good'?"
"You know what I mean."

The trip across town to Patricia Vice's campaign headquarters took over an hour. Traffic was worse than usual for that time of day. Stephanie grumbled about it, but I fielded no complaints. Cars aren't ideal for naps, but they're serviceable. I shook myself awake when Stephanie killed the engine.

Patricia Vice housed her headquarters in a two-story building which had once spent time as both a grocery store and bowling alley. Of course, the campaign had talked this up, using it as an example of Vice's commitment to urban renewal. The papers devoured it; I was a bit more skeptical.

Banners, signs, pamphlets, fliers, and myriads of other propaganda greeted us inside the converted building. A woman, wider than she was tall, looked up from her paper sorting as we approached. She wasn't ugly. Few people are truly ugly. However, the folding table she sat behind was the more interesting of the pair.

"Welcome to Representative Vice's Reelection Headquarters." The capitalization was evident. "How may I help you?"

Stephanie took the lead, launching into a spiel I couldn't repeat if I tried. The woman's smile faltered at the barrage, probably unused to being addressed in such a way, but then it was back and her voice as cheerful as ever.

"This should help." She attempted to hand Stephanie a flyer. "It discusses Representative Vice's views on all the important issues of the election."

We were dismissed. I expected it. What savvy politician would allow a simpleton to be her primary contact with the press and the public?

Stephanie ignored the pamphlet. "That might serve as a beginning, but I doubt it. Mass-produced papers never quite tell you everything. My interest lies beyond those questions found in the usual literature. Besides, it's important to understand all points of view in my line of work."

Technically, she was right. We wanted to avoid bias. But we did let the receptionist draw her own conclusions. She called over her shoulder to a gentleman with thick glasses and a too-tight tie. What followed was a game of pass the buck played by members of Vice's staff. It took over two hours and twelve different people before we found ourselves seated in front of Jeffery Hunt.

To this day, I still have no idea how Stephanie did it. Cutting through that much red tape is rarely possible. Occasionally, after a particularly satisfying meal, I'll bring it up. Sometimes she just looks at me, while others she'll throw out a scrap I never recognized as such. Last week, she told me she switched her goal from Vice to her chief of staff after learning of Vice's absence. I learned of Vice's absence when Hunt mentioned it.

Jeffery Hunt was roughly my height, in his midthirties, and wore frameless glasses and a receding hairline with equal aplomb. He sat behind a dime-store desk watching Stephanie and me in our own pair of drab chairs. Apparently, the good representative's policy on urban renewal included reducing the furniture budget. Books and papers lay scattered on every available surface of a spare table, filing cabinets, and a rickety bookshelf. I only wished they'd do something about the smell.

As we sat, Hunt made some polite mumblings, apologizing for the accommodations, but Stephanie waved them away. "I originally wished to speak to Mrs. Vice in person."

"Representative Vice"—Hunt's emphasis was plain—"is currently meeting with supporters. She isn't available and won't be for some time."

Stephanie snorted. "For a man whose profession evolved manners into an art form, you seem devoid of any basic skill. Do not interrupt me with trivialities. While Mrs. Vice may be a representative for this district, she kept her married name after the death of her husband, correct? Then I am no more improper referring to her as missus than I am calling a *Panthera Leo* a lion. They are the same, if by different names."

Hunt removed his glasses and cleaned them with a handkerchief he pulled from a pocket. "Perhaps. But in these halls, she is a representative of this fine district and should be addressed in a manner respecting the position she holds."

"The idea that respect is given without earning it is nonsense. Almost every organization realizes this. In the army, you earn rank. At your job, you earn a promotion. Yet in politics, you win a seat, and that win entitles you to respect. No, Mr. Hunt, a position in one's governmental assembly does not guarantee respect. Mind you, there is a difference between respect and civility.

"As I was saying, I originally wished to speak to Mrs. Vice in person, but I long ago learned she wouldn't be joining us today. I switched my interest to you, and here we sit." Stephanie flashed a smile that failed to touch her eyes. "Do you know a man by the name of Arthur

Swope?"

"Yes." The word was clipped. "He's a noteworthy contributor to Representative Vice's campaign. What's this have to do with us?"

"I'm looking into the death of Andrea Swope."

"Andrea?" The words came out breathy and furtive. "You're here about Andrea? I didn't know Andrea Swope very well. No one here did." Hunt sat back, eyeing both of us. Stephanie returned the look. I attempted a bored expression, switching my gaze between people and other objects in the room. When Hunt spoke again, his voice was brisk with frost forming at the edges. "I think this conversation is at an end."

"Nonsense." Stephanie's tone was of humorous insolence. "Should I leave to continue my inquiry without your input, you risk damaging your position further."

Hunt's face contorted in controlled anger, his hand outstretched and pointing to the door. "You think I don't know who you are, Mrs. Hawthorne? I know everyone who walks through that door. You barge into my office, insinuating we are connected to a murder, and don't expect us to react? You—"

I tuned Hunt out as he used words shunned by polite society.

Stephanie let him ramble before she cut him off.

She didn't yell. The word was a command which brooked no argument.

"Quiet."

Hunt shut up, seemingly of his own will save for the expression on his face. It bore a look of shock, surprised at his own compliance. Stephanie went on. "Don't be vulgar. This isn't some three-ring circus for us to entertain loutish oafs with lowbrow commentary. Do not lessen yourself, your employer, or your argument by spewing intellectual garbage.

"Use that mass of grey matter you call a brain. If you know who I am, you know what damage I can cause. If anyone wished to harm Mrs. Vice's campaign, the ammunition is already theirs. I made no attempt to hide my identity. Your best option is not to remove me but rather influence my decisions by answering questions. Now, will you answer my questions or risk making a spectacle of your candidate?"

Hunt glared at her over his glasses for a moment before easing back in his seat. Stephanie nodded as if his consent was already a foregone conclusion. To her it probably was. "What is Mr. Swope's connection with this campaign?"

"Arthur's a donor and an occasional organizer. Representative Vice trusts his opinion, as do I."

"What else?"

Hunt shot a glance out a nearby window. "That's it."

Stephanie's lips twitched. "What did he help organize?"

"Mostly high-class fundraisers. Arthur seems to know everybody who's somebody—or wants to be somebody—in this town. His connections have strengthened Representative Vice's campaign significantly."

"Mr. Swope must believe in Mrs. Vice and her bid."

"Up until his wife's premature death, he stood firmly behind Representative Vice and her platform. Only after Mrs. Swope's passing did that resolve waiver. Perhaps waiver is the wrong word. He still supports Representative Vice, just not in the same capacity as before."

"How involved was Mrs. Swope with the campaign?"

Hunt pursed his lips. "As far as I could tell, she did nothing more than she had to. She never seemed to want to be part of the campaign. If she wasn't distant and aloof, she sat and criticized everything."

"So she didn't want to be there. Then why come along?"

"You didn't know Andrea very well, did you?" Hunt shook his head. "Nobody, Arthur included, could force Andrea to do anything. She attended because she wanted to."

Hunt looked away. I followed his gaze out the window to a faded drugstore advertisement painted on the brick wall across the street. It reminded me of the eyes of God from *The Great Gatsby*. He stayed focused on it as his words floated to my ears.

"The thing is, Andrea Swope always impressed me as a society girl. If it increased her popularity or kept her in the public eye, she did it. She looked at these fundraisers the same way. Publicity stunts. Causes or people—they never meant anything to her."

"You learned this from a few fundraisers?"

"Yes. No." He paused for a second and sighed. "Occasionally, I saw her away from the paparazzi, behind closed doors when Arthur couldn't keep her away. Her distain was palpable, especially when we were the target of her ministrations. She left soon enough when she realized we wouldn't follow her orders."

"Did Mrs. Swope ever talk about her other engagements?" Stephanie asked.

Hunt turned away from the window, his face coming alive. "What else did she ever talk about? She'd go on rants about her social life—who was pissing her off and why, and which groups they were in. It only stopped when she was . . . feeling good, shall we say."

"What do you mean 'feeling good'?"

"You know what I mean." He mimed taking a drink using his hand.

"That happen often?"

Hunt snorted. "The alcohol was more than a friendly acquaintance. Hell, she was usually flat-out drunk. Whenever that happened, she would share whatever she wanted. Andrea was always more than willing to share your flaws with the rest of the world. I received that tirade more than once. It was not enjoyable."

"Did she focus her attention on a particular person or whoever was at hand?"

At this point, I started to get antsy. I knew why I was here, but sitting around listening to someone talk about a person I remembered all too well and not too fondly wasn't my idea of a good time. On a whim, I got up and strolled around the office to study the décor. Our host glanced at me before continuing. Stephanie ignored me entirely.

"She was indiscriminate, but Arthur was always her favorite subject. One night she discussed what she called the 'abomination that is our school system' before transitioning into her husband's shortcomings in the bedroom. Arthur secreted her into another room before she passed out, but not until after we all knew her opinions on the matter."

I finished my tour of the room. There wasn't much to look at. As I passed the door on the way back to my seat, a knock sounded: short, quick, and perfunctory. The door opened to admit a woman. She acknowledged our existence with a nod before speaking to Hunt.

"Jeff, we need to talk. The recent poll numbers from—"

I stepped forward, stuck out a hand, and pulled her next to me. "Representative Vice, I assume." She nodded—See? I've earned my detective license—and I turned to Stephanie. "Let me introduce you to that brunette from Swope's office."

Stephanie inclined her head a precise inch. "Greetings, Mrs. Vice."

Vice's mouth tightened before giving way to a radiant smile. "Ms. Hawthorne, it's a pleasure. Your reputation precedes you." She walked over to stand next to Hunt. "Unfortunately, I must speak privately with my chief of staff. If you two could excuse us?"

That was a dismissal. I expected Stephanie to balk, but she just stood, requesting an appointment with

Representative Vice. We were directed across the hall where I set everything up for the earliest time I could—two weeks later. Honestly, I didn't feel like it would be honored, but it was better than doing nothing. It was long after we'd left before either of us spoke up.

"That could've gone better," I said as Stephanie turned into the parking lot of a local diner.

"Actually, quite the contrary." Greetings from other regulars as we entered prevented any explanation until we took a booth in the back.

I glanced at the menu before setting it aside. Today was not a day to experiment with my stomach. "How do you figure?"

Stephanie didn't respond right away. I stared out the window. It was a nice window. The view could've used some help.

Our waitress, a red-haired beauty who could slay sausages as easily as hearts, took our order in a matter of seconds. When she left, Stephanie turned back to me. "Where were we?"

"You were about to tell me why we're not going to drop the case."

"Ah." She took a sip of coffee. "What are your thoughts on the matter?"

I explained everything as I saw it from the

beginning. Stephanie nodded as I justified my point of view, letting me wind my own way. Finally, I ran out of steam. "As I see it, the case went cold long ago. The police haven't had any new leads in weeks. Everything that could be learned from routine questions already has been. Denying that will only leave us spinning our wheels."

"You are correct about one thing: there is nothing more we can learn through routine questions that the police haven't already discovered. All we can do is form conjectures based upon what we see, disregarding the conclusions of others. We do have one thing on our side. Complacency."

Stephanie sat back, sipped her water, and explained our next steps. Soon, our food arrived. I dug into a roast beef on rye while Stephanie poked at her soup.

The rest of the meal didn't pass in silence, but the conversation was personal. Suffice it to say, we experienced laughter and merriment. We may be a detective company, and she may be the boss, but we were also a couple. It was nice to reaffirm it.

Chapter 6

"Everything is clear if we only stand in the right place."

Stephanie had no post-meal instructions for me, so I took on the responsibility of our next steps. I sat behind the wheel, the day's events running through my mind, finally speaking up about a mile from the office. "Something's getting to me. Everyone says Andrea switched charities whenever her mood shifted, leaving chaos in her wake. These groups must have known about her tendency to do so, yet they welcomed her with open arms. Why? There has to be more to it than what Robert said."

Stephanie stared out the front window with a hint of a smile. "I agree. Why willingly introduce chaos into a balanced system?"

I pulled into a random driveway to turn the car around. "Then let's go ask."

"No." The word was quiet yet firm. "Home. I want to return home."

Home. She only called it home when her plans were personal. In all other things—business or otherwise—she referred to it as the office. Had she said office, I wouldn't have questioned it. But she hadn't.

Putting the car in park, I looked at her. "There are things which need doing. Going home is not among them." I knew my voice sounded condescending, but I didn't care.

"No. Home." Stephanie stared straight ahead with her arms crossed. If she acted like a spoiled child, I'd treat her as such. I put the car in gear and backed out.

I refuse to call that afternoon a bust, but it definitely wasn't a success. The first charity I pulled from our list couldn't tell us much we hadn't already heard. Nor could any of the other organizations. By three o'clock, faces blurred but still recited the same sentiments. At four o'clock, I vowed never to admit that I once dated Andrea. By five, I felt ready to lead the enraged masses to string her up in effigy.

All accounts agreed. It seemed Andrea's modus operandi was to appear, proclaim her importance, and, waving money around, gain influence over the organization. Then she changed everything to fit her whims, only to disappear when she got bored. This left the organization high and dry, dependent upon her input and money. She repeated the same tactic over and over, again and again.

Had the organizations warned each other? Yes, though few listened, while even fewer still heeded the warnings. Andrea's money and influence proved too much to resist. Whichever group she supported at that time sat gloriously triumphant above the rest. Such heights only made the fall from grace all the harder. Robert seemed to be right, as much as that truth irked me.

Of course, had Stephanie chosen to participate, our results might have changed. At the first charity, a local food pantry, Stephanie refused to leave the car. Rather than arguing, I went in without her. I emerged half an hour later to find her reading one of those damn romance novels she was addicted to, her seat reclined as far as it would go. Whenever she avoided work in favor of something else, she appeared like a spoiled child rather than the professional she claimed to be. Climbing in, I shared this opinion and was summarily ignored. This pattern held through the rest of my visits.

I saved the animal shelter for last, it being the of the most obvious use. Only there did Stephanie put down her book and deign to join me as I walked toward the sprawling one-story structure. It felt too little too late, but it was better than her ignoring the case at hand.

Inside, the building resembled an old elementary school from my childhood. The cinder block walls were painted the same off-white and sickly green colors. Three bookcases filled with training pamphlets were augmented by a dozen industrial chairs in a faded orange hue and a single, fake, potted plant. Dog and cat smells filled the air. It was a persistent odor, but not an unpleasant one. Such was to be expected. What we didn't expect was the fervent greeting we received from an overly friendly female Great Dane.

After successfully defending myself from the onslaught of her tongue, I held up wet hands and looked at Stephanie. She stood to one side, arms crossed in disapproval. Before we entered, I heard her mumbling to herself about the order in which I chose to visit the organizations. She thought I had wasted time. You already know my opinion on the situation. We shared a sense of annoyance, if for different reasons. I decided to do something about it. My hands were wet. Her shirt was dry.

I remedied the situation.

Just as Stephanie pulled away, a petite, raven-haired beauty entered the room. She appeared overdressed for an animal shelter. Still, she looked good. Her face bore almond eyes and full lips that curled into a smile. There was an attraction about her my loins found hard to resist. Her eyes smoldered as she took me in, and I felt weak-kneed as she locked her eyes on mine.

"May I help you?"

I tried to speak, but my tongue fused to the roof of my mouth. My jaw worked, but nothing came out. Stephanie stepped into the awkward silence.

"I would like to talk to Mrs. Helen Swope." Her voice was back to its professional tone, all traces of sulkiness gone. I knew better.

Our hostess smiled and not in a friendly way. "The great Stephanie Hawthorne. You took longer than I expected. But now that you're here, we can proceed. Follow me."

We did so. Dogs barked behind closed doors as we made our way through the halls. She led us into a small office the size of a broom closet with everything jammed in with no particular order. The desk could have used a new lacquer job, while the two chairs which sat before it were worn and obviously as secondhand as the desk. A handful of framed documents and pictures hung from pockmarked walls. Our host looked incongruous behind that desk. Taking a seat, I reflected on how many desks I'd sat in front of over the past twelve hours. I was ready for the day to end.

"Who would have thought it? Stephanie Hawthorne coming to see me. I can only assume you're here about my late mother-in-law." A knowing smile formed on our host's lips.

"I take it you are Mrs. Swope?" Stephanie was as formal as ever.

"Please, Mrs. Swope was my mother-in-law. Call me Helen. We don't stand much on formality here."

Stephanie grunted. "I do."

"Doesn't that make things a bit confusing? I won't know which one of us you're referring to."

"I find it impossible to believe you are that simpleminded. Shall I repeat the question?"

Helen—I had no problem with the name—shook her head. "Helen Black. Ms. Black, if you insist. As I said, Mrs. Swope was my mother-in-law."

"Semantics. You are married; therefore, the moniker *missus* applies to you in your situation. If the title fits, it may be applied."

Helen pursed her lips. "I see two problems with your assessment. First, referring to a woman by her husband's last name is an outdated rule. It was developed in a male dominated society to show ownership of said woman. Our sex can now own property, develop businesses, and run governments without the need for a penis. I think we can overcome the necessity of adopting our husbands' surnames.

"Secondly, in order for me to be Mrs. Helen

Swope, I need to have a legal right to the name. This means Swope is a name I accepted, recognized, and adopted, usually requiring a court decree or a marriage. I never adopted nor accepted that name, instead choosing to continue carrying my birth name to my marriage bed every night. Black is my last name."

Suddenly I felt sorry for Robert. Not only did he have Andrea for a mother and a demanding father, but now to find him married to such a woman was almost too much. Granted, Stephanie was similar, but . . .

To hell with that. Stephanie was exactly the same.

"Mrs. Black then. Did you—"

Our host interrupted again. "That was my mother. Helen."

Stephanie shook her head. "Describe your relationship with the late Mrs. Swope."

Helen made a disapproving noise with her tongue. "I'm sorry, but no. I never agreed to answer any of your questions."

"Then why bring us back here? Are you trying to be as infuriating as possible?"

"Everything is clear if we only stand in the right place. From where I sit," Helen gestured around herself, "my motives are obvious. It's all about perspective. For example, why are you here? No, don't answer. It's more entertaining to guess."

Stephanie crossed her arms. "Guess? You know precisely why I am here, yet you are cantankerous at every turn. Why?"

Helen's lips twisted in amusement. "Perhaps I have some dark secret to hide. Perhaps I just find it entertaining."

"Every charity involved with Mrs. Swope eventually regretted the decision. All save this one. Here, she never attempted to take over, let alone succeeded in doing so. She left other charities out of boredom or frustration after mere weeks or months. Here, she spent years. I want to know why."

"She loved all the pussies. Excuse me, cats." Helen giggled, and not in a friendly manner. "The dogs, too. Dear mom-in-law really had a soft spot for all the little creatures of the world. Just couldn't stand to see one go unloved. She lavished attention on each and every one."

Helen paused, tapping her lips with a finger before continuing. "As for her taking over, I wouldn't let her. This place is mine. I created it and I will oversee it. No one will take that from me." Her eyes burned hot with that last statement. For an instant, she looked more a cobra than a woman. Then it was gone and a smile graced her features as she sat back.

Stephanie had apparently had enough. She stood and headed for the door with me in tow but stopped in the doorway. "What do you know about Mrs. Swope's jewelry?"

"It boils down to money. It always does." I couldn't see Helen, but the sneer in her voice was hardly hidden. "Jewelry—opulence designed to flatter the vain and disguise the poor. I don't know a damn thing about it."

Stephanie stalked off, shoes clicking down the empty hallway. I followed.

Chapter 7

"You don't have to entice me. That body didn't hurt your case."

Silence dominated the ride back to the office. Helen Black's comments caused me to set aside my usual banter. Something about that woman rubbed me wrong—rubbed us wrong. Part of me wanted to discuss everything, but my gut warned me off, as if mentioning her was akin to summoning her.

Upon exiting the building, Stephanie had said exactly one sentence. "That is a very dangerous woman."

She wasn't frightened—that much I could tell—but unnerved. I could see it in her face, by the set of her jaw and the wrinkles working on her forehead. Granted, she might have snowballed me, but I didn't think so. It wasn't her style. But at least she ignored her book. That was a good sign.

The sun sat low in the sky when we arrived back at the office. Stephanie went upstairs—to start dinner, I hoped—while I went into the office to check for messages before closing down for the night.

Night had fallen by the time I made it upstairs.

Stephanie sat in the darkness, curled in a recliner with her feet drawn up beneath her and her head propped on her hand. She stared at a blank TV screen. I ignored her and flipped on the kitchen light to start dinner. Halfway through the culinary battle, Stephanie appeared at the door, a ladder-back chair in hand. She straddled the chair, placing her arms along the back and resting her chin on her forearms.

"This murder's a conundrum." As she spoke, her head bobbed up and down. It amused me more than it should have. "There are pieces, fractions of the truth, but nothing remotely close to a lead. Only more questions."

"I doubt I can help," I said. "You're the brains of the operation, not me. I just file paperwork and drive you places." Anger flittered across Stephanie's face, and I hurried on. "But if you want a sounding board, go on and I'll add as I can."

Stephanie glared at me through narrowed eyes. I would pay for that comment sooner or later. "What's your opinion of that woman?"

She meant Helen. It seemed petty to deny a name, but I let it lie. "I don't know. My gut tells me she may know something, but whether it's the identity of a murderer or the location of D.B. Cooper, I have no idea."

"That woman spoke in riddles." Stephanie sighed.

"No, not riddles. Hints and allegations, but not riddles. Purposely disguising interests and motives for gain is understandable, but this seemed solely for enjoyment. She intentionally tried to confound us, but she lacks the understanding that uncovering a person's motives and actions is not a sprint, but a marathon."

I added some garlic and paprika to the sauce in the pan. "That might be so, but it stymies us in the short term. Though it fit with the rest of the afternoon. What bothers me is that no one seems to have the same opinion of Andrea." I dropped a couple chicken breasts into the sauce. "There was a general consensus, but opinions ran the gamut from devotion to hatred."

Stephanie moved into the kitchen and stood behind me. I could hear dishes clinking behind my back. "Not quite. The question is how much was a show for our benefit? Take me, for example. I'm quite aware of the impression I give the general public, yet you not only accepted it but chose matrimony. This implies a greater depth of character within myself than is readily apparent. The same may hold true for Mrs. Swope. She had her vices and demons, her ambitions and desires. Yet whatever they were, I suspect nothing as simple as publicity."

"Your lips speak of depth of character, yet I know you said yes in part so someone could drop your ego a peg or two when needed." Stephanie crossed her arms and cocked her hip. In for a penny, in for a pound. "You don't have to entice me. That body didn't hurt your case."

Stephanie continued, trying to maintain an air of self-righteous indignation from beside the silverware she'd set on the dining room table. "Obvious reasons fit the persona Mrs. Swope presented, but I highly doubt that is anywhere near the truth. A few points require clarification. That seems as good a place to start as any."

The next morning, I found myself revisiting most of the charities from the day before. Sometimes the person I spoke to recognized me, making my task much easier— not that much opposition existed. Most wished to be free of Andrea's legacy, making them more than willing to share. All save for a few of the stops lasted a matter of minutes, with even the more difficult encounters requiring only a little extra persuasion.

I was delighted to find Helen Black absent when I stopped by the animal shelter. Something beyond Stephanie's comments warned me off that woman. My instincts screamed at me long before Stephanie said a single word. But the young woman I dealt with was pleasant and everything Helen was not.

By noon, I had finished and returned to the office. Save for myself, the building sat empty, this time with

Stephanie disappearing to the local library where she sponsored a knitting circle. It seemed to be a hit with high school girls. That made little sense, until I started to consider their topics of conversation. Oh, the stories Stephanie could tell! I shrugged it off. Besides, young women could have worse role models.

Stephanie returned two hours later, just as I finished my task of compiling a list of budget expenditures during Andrea's tenure with each charity. It seemed Andrea repeated the same five functions over and over again at each organization, with little or no variation. Each event seemed to cost the same, and none of it came from within existing budgets.

I handed Stephanie the data and sat in bored silence as she perused it all. It was such a stimulating experience that I became more engrossed by my leg falling asleep than by Stephanie's reactions.

Finally, she spoke up. "You're sure this is everything?"

I nodded. "All that I could get. Most groups wouldn't give up more than that, citing privacy issues. Anything there?"

"No, but I had to be sure. It appears most places kept Mrs. Swope away from the purse strings, if barely so. That, combined with her husband's apparent wealth, makes greed an unlikely motivation."

"Wait." I held up a hand, ticking off points on my fingers. "Two things. First, we know why Andrea bounced between charities: publicity. If it wasn't that, then what? We have no better working hypothesis, so I vote we stay with it.

"Second, what do you mean 'apparent wealth?' The man owns and runs a multimillion-dollar law firm. I checked. The wealth exists."

Stephanie shook her head. "Never trust the obvious. With it, people see what they want but seldom see the truth it hides. I don't believe Mrs. Swope assisted those charities just for the limelight. Yes, she might have enjoyed it, but I doubt it was a primary motivation.

"As for Mr. Swope's wealth, if he is so rich, why was all of Mrs. Swope's jewelry paste and colored glass? Better yet, how did her murderer know to avoid it?" Suddenly, Stephanie smacked her desk. "Curse that ex-girlfriend of yours. Why'd she have to drag us into this confounded mess?"

"I don't think she had much to do with it. That agreement was between you and her late husband. She seemed to be a bit preoccupied with being dead when you took on the case. Don't glare at me. What's next?"

Stephanie's scowl relaxed not a millimeter as she

spoke. "This information removes any hope I had of a credible lead. Now we must rely on assumptions and surmises."

I shrugged. "Fine by me, but we'll need proof to get Swope to pay out."

"Undoubtedly. I hoped to stir up the proverbial pot with our questioning. But with nothing but guesses since our start twenty-four hours ago, I cannot expect action quite so soon. People hold secrets close to their hearts—doubly so for the guilty. Someone is guilty, but to prove who, we must pry them loose."

"Is this what you call an assumption?" Perhaps my tone was more mocking than I intended.

Stephanie snarled like a cornered tiger. "Get out of your ivory tower. Everyone has secrets. It's one of the many facets which make us human. Ferreting out those secrets is the nature of our profession." She kept her glare on me for a heartbeat or two before returning to the report. I turned to other paperwork. Silence lay heavy about the room for the next two hours.

Which was fine by me.

Oddly enough, it was Stephanie who spoke first. "I saw Jenny today." Jennifer Winters was my sister's youngest child and the baby of the family. "She's doing well."

At the mention of my niece, I felt a pit open up in my stomach. Something told me I wasn't going to like where this was headed. Jennifer had graduated from high school the previous spring and originally intended to go on to college. But recently those ideas had started to change. Maybe now I'd find out why.

"Where'd you see her?" I tried to hide my anxiety.

Stephanie looked up from her reading. "She attended class today. You know she usually does. Apparently, college is officially off."

"That's nuts. She's a bright girl. Factory work would be wasted on a brain like hers."

"She isn't thinking of factory work." Stephanie said it in that way people have when they want you to ask a question but don't want to come out and say it.

"Stephanie, what's going on?"

My wife's face went blank. No, I wasn't going to like this one bit. "Perhaps she could help us out. Gain a little experience before she starts out on her own."

"What're you talking about?"

I got an exasperated look for my efforts. "What experience can only we offer? She intends to become a private detective."

Click. Clack. Clunk. The key turned and the door opened. Nope, I didn't like it one bit. "No."

"Daniel. She's family."

"Don't care. Not going to happen."

Stephanie scolded me. "We could use the help and she wants the experience."

I could tell she was annoyed that I didn't immediately agree with her. The way she saw it, Watson always deferred to Sherlock, and I should do the same. And in most circumstances, she'd be right. I let her boss me around; it was how the business worked. But this time was different—family was involved. There was no way I wanted my niece involved in any case. Maybe that sentiment was a bit naïve, but I intended to protect Jennifer. This was not the life for her.

For the next half hour, we went around in circles. Stephanie tried to convince me of the merits, while I stubbornly held my position. She cited experience. I mentioned education. She decried the system. I reminded her that we all had to be licensed. Finally, she crossed her arms and glared at me over them.

"Well, what do you suggest? I'm considering searching ground already covered by the police in all their masses. There's no other viable option, unless you want me to divine the murderer through tarot cards."

"Then try that."

Stephanie threw up her hands. "Do you think I'm

unaware of this? Just because my familial bonds lack strength does not mean I am unaware of them in others. I'll keep it easy because she *is* family and because she *is* untested. What I have planned for her is so simple a trained baboon could perform it."

Stephanie outlined her plans for Jennifer. She was to tail a select few of our recent acquaintances. The job didn't have to be subtle. In fact, Stephanie wanted the opposite. Jennifer was to upset the status quo. Should it succeed, we'd have a new lead. Most importantly to me, it could convince my niece that detective work wasn't her cup of proverbial tea.

Of course, Jennifer loved the idea.

Chapter 8

"You know, it would take only a matter of minutes to call—"

Over the next three days, I instructed Jennifer on the ins and outs of basic detective work, spending the vast majority of my time focusing on the nuts and bolts of tailing. Jennifer was an average-sized young woman with straight blonde hair and a set of piercing blue eyes. A strong, quick mind hid behind what I could objectively call a beautiful face and a shapely body—which I knew for a fact could outrun most people, thanks to years on the school's track team. More than once, I'd threatened to join her father in cleaning his guns when prospective suitors came to call.

However, nothing she experienced before had prepared her for this. Contrary to Stephanie's beliefs, tailing is more an art than a science. Perhaps that explains why I'm much better at it than she. A good bit was training, repeating the same skills over and over again until they become instinct. But tailing has a flip side. Sometimes actions can't be predicted by anything except your gut. You need to know when to listen to it. Stephanie never really understood that.

By the end of the first day, Jennifer had perfected countless skills in the what-not-to-do category. Despite an urge to just stop outright, I pressed on, refusing to have my niece start out unprepared. Therefore, I set out to fix those problems on the second day. By noon, Jennifer finally started to grasp everything I had harped on the day before, so we moved on to making other mistakes. I found myself more than a little sore, both physically and mentally, by the time we called it quits. Yet I knew one thing—Jennifer showed talent.

On the third day, we started from the beginning and reviewed the basics. As a kid, my parents had beaten into my head some maxim about practicing. I don't remember the words, but the lesson stuck. So that was what Jennifer and I did. We started at eight in the morning, and by ten she was bored. At noon she wanted to stop. When three rolled around, I finally gave her an ultimatum: either do it again or go home and forget about the job. She shut up and we continued.

At five, Jennifer got cocky. Truth be told, she had progressed a long way. After three days, her natural talent had shown through, even with all her problems. However, her own opinion of her skills was a bit too high. She needed some of the wind taken out of her sails. Even the best detective can lose a mark, no matter how good they are, and she needed to realize that. Before quitting for the night, I challenged her to tail me from the far end of downtown back to the office. I'll spare you the details, but it only ended when I tapped her on the shoulder. After following her for five blocks.

So we started again. On the way back to our starting point, I explained what she did wrong and she nodded, absorbing it as best as she could. I had time for one final lesson. We switched roles, with her trying to lose me. She started off, and I hailed a cab to take me back to the office. Jennifer looked all cocky until she saw me eating a sandwich at my desk. I'll let you figure out the lesson.

The next day, Stephanie got the green light to send Jennifer out on her own, and we both dove into our individual tasks. Stephanie ordered Jennifer to tail specific people until she was called off. I never learned the rhyme or reason behind the chosen order, but I suspected one existed.

During that time, I started piecing together Andrea's regular weekly and monthly habits. Unfortunately, no pattern emerged as I did so, save for four specific events outside of her charitable endeavors. I quickly ruled them out. The only option left required a visit to the animal shelter. I was loath to do this since I didn't want to run into Helen again. Even so, I had mixed feelings when Stephanie nixed my visit the night before I was supposed to go.

The next morning, a Wednesday, I found myself standing before the Swope house. I rang the bell three times and waited five minutes before letting myself in. Stephanie had already warned Swope of my arrival, so I wasn't worried about the police showing up. The red heels Stephanie admired still sat beneath the hallway table. They were the obvious reason Stephanie sent me, and I decided for the twelve-millionth time that she needed to work on her fashion sense. Picking them up, I headed into the kitchen.

Now that I wasn't following Stephanie around, I paused for a minute to examine the room. It was one of those combined kitchen and dining rooms. An eight-foot-long island tiled in black and white stood before me, a built-in stove jutting out of it. Behind it, matching tile work covered twelve acres of counter which held everything from the microwave to a knife block that sat beside the sink. Recessed lighting gave the room a modern feel, while the stark, white walls created a sense of emptiness. Nothing individualized it. To my left, a bare bay window framed the oblong kitchen table and its matching chairs.

The cat still sat in the same place as our last visit. She blinked at me, and I acknowledged her in kind. Everything in the room seemed exactly the same, including the empty water dish. I filled it at the sink.

Unlike Stephanie, however, I lack the grace of a dancer and somehow managed to knock the knife block into the sink. Maybe I brushed it as I moved to fill the water dish, or perhaps it was already positioned precariously and the wind from my passing sent it over the edge. All I know is, one minute it was fine and the next the sink was a dangerous prospect.

That proved to be more than enough excitement for the cat, which, at the sudden noise, bolted for parts unknown. My shoulders slumped. That's what happens when I try to do a good deed. After filling the water dish, I dried the knives on a nearby towel and slid them back into their notches. They were all high quality and well treated. So it struck me as odd when I found a good half inch missing from the tip of a butcher knife. It stuck in my mind while I finished with the other knives and returned to my task.

I don't know what possessed me, but I mounted the stairs, taking the steps two at a time. Everything seemed to be in the same state as during my previous visit.

I followed my gut into the master bedroom. Nothing here had changed, either.

Standing in the doorway, I just looked. It's harder than you think. Try it sometime; pick a place and study it. You'll see all the flaws and imperfections which make a place unique. See all the little ticks and quirks which develop. Focus on those things and you'll learn about you and me and everyone else.

As I stood there, Stephanie's comments from that morning ran through my head. "I highly doubt that anything tangible will be left now that the police have finished. Instead, focus on abnormalities. Assume her lifestyle was a façade she wished to maintain lest anyone discover her true motives. We must draw that curtain aside. I don't expect this to be a simple task; otherwise it would have been done already. If she has, in fact, been hiding things for years, it will not have been clumsily done.

"But no man, woman, or child is perfect. Mistakes are made, mistakes we must capitalize upon. They could have been made by anyone. You know how to look for these things. Find them. Any crevasse we pry open might be important. I'll give you one thing: those red heels. Bring them back to me."

Again, nothing stood out. I knew what the closet held, the dresser, and all the miniscule places people traditionally hid their secrets. Leaning against the doorframe, I closed my eyes to think. I needed to rip everything away and start fresh. Andrea wasn't a stupid woman. Bigoted and hostile, yes, but not stupid. Nothing important would be hidden where others could easily access it. That ruled out all the furniture, which I had already discarded. What was left?

Nothing. That was the problem. The floorboards were the only things left, but hiding secrets below them was more a movie trick than anything found in real life. Still, I had to rule them out. I dropped to my knees and examined the floor for over an hour, searching everywhere including inside the bed frame. A giant goose egg.

I sat back on my heels and glared at the groove cut out of the floorboards. Slowly it dawned on me that something glittered in the sunlight streaming in from the window. Placing my nose only a handful of inches from the groove, I felt along its length with my fingers, first one way and then another. Nothing seemed unusual, yet I knew I'd seen something. Closing my eyes, I concentrated on the sensations from my fingertips as I sent them over the wood again.

That's when I felt it.

A sliver of metal sat jammed into the floor that my finding it seemed more luck than anything else. It was imbedded so deep that I had to shift to my right to get the light perfect before I was able to see it.

I had an idea and made a beeline to the kitchen, grabbing the suspect butcher knife from the block. Back in the bedroom, I compared the two pieces of metal. They matched, as near as I could tell. Now what? James would need to know, but Stephanie came first. But what to do in the meantime? The evidence seemed hidden well enough for now, having survived the past six months undiscovered. Odds were it would survive another day or two.

From where I sat eyeing the bullet groove, I had a straight line view beneath the dresser. Hidden under a thick layer of dust lay a tiny piece of paper—folded or crumpled up, depending on your point of view. I fished about before drawing it out. Dust swirled out along with it, resulting in a sneezing fit which lasted the better part of a minute. Dusting under dressers was obviously not high on the cleaning service's priority list.

Unfolding it, I recognized the yellow carbon half of a receipt from the local dry cleaner's Stephanie and I frequented. The establishment's name, Jake's, spanned the top of the paper, along with its address and phone number. Someone had scrawled an illegible word across the bottom, in the space designed for notes, along with a phone number and a date of almost a year ago. An identification number inked in red scored the top corner of the page.

I stuffed the paper into my pocket and scanned the room again. It may not be important, but then again, it could be.

Grabbing the knife from beside the gouge, I left the room more than a little annoyed. For several days, I had traipsed around town on a fruitless hunt with nothing more to show for it than sore feet and an empty tank of gas. Now we had a lead, but instead of being thrilled, I wanted to scream at my wife. Stephanie had obviously suspected something, yet she'd supplied me with no more direction than "go there and look."

Here's the thing. Taken as a whole, criminals aren't that smart. Most lack the forethought required to create a successful ending. Crimes of opportunity and passion rarely allow for the moments of clarity needed for a criminal to evade capture.

Preplanned crimes are a different matter entirely. Forethought, patience, and sustained malice toward others are required while the criminal waits for the perfect opportunity to strike. These people are often sociopaths, which is why those crimes are prosecuted with such zeal.

Everything about this crime denoted preparation.

Everything—from the missing bullet to the position of the body to the vaguest hint of a robbery—indicated that the murderer knew exactly what steps to take. That created a central question which consumed my attention: why kill Andrea Swope?

Despite my current desire to avoid Stephanie, I needed to report in. I returned the knife to the kitchen and found a wall-mounted phone. It seemed like something from a bygone era, but a dial tone sounded in my ear. After dialing the number I knew best, I waited a series of rings before an overly cheerful voice answered.

"Stephanie Hawthorne's office." She never introduced herself. That way she could deny availability to anyone to whom she didn't wish to speak.

"It's me. I'm finished up here, but I found something. I'm going to check on it now.

She dropped the act. "What is it?"

I gave her all of it—the whole story from start to finish. Stephanie didn't interrupt as I spilled the beans. When I finished I expected instructions, and she didn't disappoint. "Follow up on the receipt. After that, return home. We'll work on the phone number tomorrow."

"What about the knife?"

Stephanie grunted. "Leave it. I'll have to think on it for a bit."

I shook my head. "You know, it would only take a matter of minutes to call—"

"No. I suspect things may improve soon. Should you inform James, we'll lose the night at the very least."

I sighed. "All right. I'll see you soon."

"Good." She paused and softened her tone. "Daniel, thank you."

It was my turn to grunt. "I'll see you at home."

Hanging up, I exited via the front door, taking the red shoes with me.

Chapter 9

"Questions come next. Always more questions."

The weather outside surprised me as I left the confines of the house. A chill wind buffeted me, knocking me back a step. A storm front hung over the house, creating a line of black clouds against lighter ones. Rain fell in dark lines between the clouds and the ground. The first drop hit the top of my head, and I shivered as I ducked into the car.

As I settled myself behind the wheel, water pelted the windshield, coming fast and furious. Soon, it was an all-out downpour. Feeling smug about managing to stay dry, I turned the engine over and pulled out of the driveway.

That smugness was short-lived. On the drive over to the dry cleaner's, I remembered Jennifer. With the way that morning had been, odds were that she was in the rain without even a jacket. Sadly enough, my inner self hoped this would convince her that private detective work wasn't for her.

But knowing my niece, she'd have checked the

weather and prepared for it. She inherited that from my sister. The roll of the genetic die blessed my sister and her children with the power of forethought. I wasn't bitter; I was the cuter sibling.

It was still pouring when I pulled to a stop across the street from Jake's, its *Open* sign glowing red and blue. A sodden woman attempted to hide from the rain by standing beneath the eaves of a nearby building. Inside, I saw one of the owners, Mr. Wood, talking to a woman wearing a long coat and carrying an umbrella. I unlocked the doors, reached across to the passenger-side window, and rapped on it with my knuckles. Moments later, the door opened and my niece, soaked to the skin, climbed in with the chill wind.

I turned up the heater. "That should help."

"A towel would help, Unc."

"You want out?"

Jennifer shook her head, a look of horror on her face. I reached into the back, grabbed a blanket I stored there in case of emergencies, and handed it to her. She took it gratefully and wrapped it around herself.

"Thank you," she mumbled.

"Welcome. What else do you expect me to do for my least favorite niece?"

She looked indignant. "I'm your only niece."

I shrugged.

"You know your jokes get less and less funny each time you open your mouth." It wasn't a question.

"With age comes staleness." I looked across the street. Wood had disappeared into the back, leaving the woman alone. "Who's in there?"

Jennifer used a corner of the blanket to dry her hair. "Helen Black."

I raised an eyebrow. Not who I expected. "How long have you been standing in the rain?"

"Since it started raining." I shot my niece a look and she rolled her eyes. "Only a few minutes, I think. Not sure." Jennifer looked sheepish at the admission and then nodded in Helen's direction. "She took the bus from that animal shelter and walked here from Grimes Avenue. I didn't want to pull my phone out to check the time."

I held up my arm. "Wristwatch. Did she notice you?"

"No idea. Probably." I shot her another look. She knew better than that. "Aunt Steph said I didn't have to be subtle, so I wasn't."

"That's no excuse for carelessness. Don't guess. Know."

Wood reappeared and handed Helen a red dress wrapped in the cleaner's plastic sheath. She took it in a huff and left the store, hurrying off toward Michigan and the bus stop. Jennifer returned the blanket to the backseat and grabbed the door handle.

I grabbed her arm before she could get out. "Just follow her to the bus stop. Let me know which route she takes, but don't follow her. I've got to do something, and then I'll pick you up there. Don't press your luck. Got it?" Jennifer nodded. "Good. Once more into the breach."

I got out as well, pausing despite the torrent. "And Jennifer. Good job so far."

She smiled. It was a beam of sunshine on a sodden afternoon. "Thanks, Unc." Then she was gone.

Cold water ran down my neck as I crossed the street alone. Since I knew Andre Wood personally, I had to be a bit more diplomatic than my usual methods allowed. I didn't rush across the street, but didn't dawdle either. Vents spewed cold air as I entered, goose bumps forming on my skin.

Mr. Wood looked up from the counter as I entered. He was a tall, thin man with skin as dark as pitch. A grin spread across his haggard face, showing off pearl-white teeth. While his age was a mystery to me, Jack Wood refused to bow to the demands of age. A hand shot out in greeting, and I grasped it. It was about as firm as could be without inflicting pain on its recipient.

"Mr. Atwell, good to see you. How's Mrs. Atwell?"

I didn't correct him—I never did. There was no future in it. "Stephanie's doing fine." Pulling the damp receipt from my pocket, I handed it to him. "Got a couple questions about this. What can you tell me about it?"

He gave me a knowing smile. "On the hunt for the mysteries of the universe again?"

"No, just other people's mysteries."

Wood chuckled. "That's much better. Less chance to anger The Big Guy that way. Give me a moment."

He took the receipt and squinted at the number before pecking it into a computer he had on the counter. I watched silently as he read the results before reaching below the counter and pulling out a wastepaper bin.

Picking out a particularly crumpled slip of paper, he looked at it before handing it to me. The paper matched the carbon I'd handed over. "It just left the shop."

My gut twisted. Not that it was particularly unexpected. "What was it?"

"A red dress. Quite nice actually. We don't get many items like that."

"For the record, what do you mean by just left? As in, left with the woman who was here just before me?"

Wood nodded. "That would be what I mean. Pretty but short tempered. Unhappy that I had to go and find it, too. Leave it here for as long as you did, be happy that it's still around, I say. If it hadn't been prepaid, woulda been gone a long time ago."

Wood kept talking, but I tuned him out. Catching up with Jennifer became a priority, regardless of Stephanie's instructions. I turned to go, but as I did so, something caught my attention. I turned back. "Repeat that?"

He shrugged, more than a bit annoyed at himself. "I'm sorry I can't be of more help, Mr. Atwell. I can't remember who she said she was."

Best to soothe the ruffled feathers. "That's all right. But it wasn't what I was talking about." I headed toward the door, not really wanting to waste any more time. "You said she was picking it up for a friend?"

"Right. But I can't remember that name either. I got no head for names."

"People tend to remember more than they realize." I suggested a name, and his eyes lit up.

"That's it. How'd you know?"

"Lucky guess. Thank you." I left, trudging back into the rain.

Stephanie wanted to goad someone into action.

She'd succeeded, but I doubt it was who topped her list. It definitely wasn't who I thought. Now we had to take advantage of the break.

I considered running down the street after Helen and Jennifer, but quickly nixed the urge. It seemed unlikely I would reach them in a reasonable amount of time. Besides, the rain made driving a more alluring option.

A few seconds later, with the heater set on high, I started down the street after the two women. I scanned the sidewalk as I drove but saw no one until I reached Michigan and turned right toward the bus stop. Jennifer stood huddled under a stunted tree near the bus stop sign. Someone in too much of a hurry honked as I pulled up.

Jennifer climbed in, and I handed her the blanket for a second time. "She get on the bus?"

My niece shivered and shook her head. "No. Two blocks back, she got into a black sedan. She knew exactly where it was. Walked right up and got in with no trouble."

"Don't suppose you remember the plate number?"

Jennifer beamed. "Knew you were going to ask." She held up her left arm for me. I had missed it as she climbed into the car, but now I could see a series of numbers and letters, only slightly blurred, written across the inside of her arm. With the other hand she held a

Sharpie.

A chuckle escaped me. "So what now?"

Jennifer gave me the look at which all teenage girls are much too skilled. "Aren't you supposed to be the experienced detective, O Teacher Mine?"

"I do know. I want to know if you do." Looking over my shoulder, I pulled back into traffic. "Don't get cocky. This is part of your training."

Jennifer sighed but gave in. "Okay. No idea. What's next?"

"It's rhetorical. Questions come next. Always more questions. Was the car parked in that spot when you passed by the first time?"

"I don't know. Maybe."

"You should. You need to be aware of your surroundings. Were you followed in turn? Did she know she was being followed?" Jennifer shrugged and looked at her lap, pouting. I went on. "These are things you need to be aware of. This isn't a game."

"I know it's not a game." Anger glinted in her eyes.

"Then listen and learn." I know I sounded harsh, but I was serious about this. "If you insist on doing this, I want you to do it right. You have more to worry about than I do—not only because of my age and experience, but because you're an attractive young woman. People will underestimate you, try to take advantage of you, hurt you. You can't give them the opportunity.

"Odds are the car was there. If it hadn't been, you would've seen some sign of her trying to find it—either by actively searching or calling to make the meet. It all could've been prearranged, but I don't think so. In weather like this, it would've been tricky to find a parking spot at exactly the right time on an already crowded street.

"But why not have it pick her up at the dry cleaner's? Because someone probably wanted to confirm Helen's tail, and now they know Helen had an unwelcome follower. Normally that goes against the grain, but in this case, we actually wanted that. I'm just not thrilled with someone we can't identify knowing our movements. They can make our job harder. You following?"

Jennifer nodded. "Got it."

I smiled, attempting to lessen the sting of my tirade. "Good. The next step is simple. Where did you leave your car?"

"At your place. Aunt Steph thought it better I take the bus than drive."

"Please tell me she gave you fare."

"Yep. Too much, actually. Does she ever ride the bus?"

"Not unless she's forced to." I sighed. "Which has been a good ten years or more."

"Ah." Jennifer looked out the window at the rain as it continued to pour. "Where to, then?"

"First, you buckle up. Then we head home."

The ride back seemed to fly, due in large part to my pleasant conversation with Jennifer. Although I'd seen my niece regularly over the past few days, we'd talked little about anything other than business. We fixed that.

Life seemed normal for a newly minted high school graduate. Two or three of Jennifer's friends had already had their graduation parties, but she had chosen to forgo one. There was no sign of a romantic attachment either, since she had called it quits with her longtime beau last February. Jennifer seemed content with it, saying she wanted to focus on her education, but personal experience told me how fast that opinion could change.

It was pretty standard stuff until she opened up about her problems, and I became the sympathetic shoulder. Since the beginning of her senior year, her parents and most of her extended family had been pushing her to attend a university to continue her studies. She didn't like the idea and had agreed only to keep them quiet. Then the scholarships and opportunities started rolling in, and things only became worse. By the time she graduated, she wanted nothing to do with college but had refused to say anything until recently so as not to hurt anyone's feelings.

I sympathized in a way. Not having any children of our own, Jennifer, more than any other niece or nephew, had become a surrogate child for Stephanie and me. Even though I still disagreed with her interest in private detective work, I understood her motives. I told her as much. We would still love and support her no matter what her choice. That seemed to mollify her as we pulled into the driveway behind the office.

Chapter 10

"And the heels?"

"That should be obvious."

"Pretend that it's not."

Thanks to the clouds, it was fully dark as I shut off the car. Jennifer accepted my invitation for a warm shower and a dry set of clothes and ran upstairs. She knew where everything was, so I left her to it and headed to the office. I paused at the door for a moment before entering. My footsteps echoed as I came up behind Stephanie who sat in her chair facing the window.

"Jennifer's upstairs." Stephanie nodded and I went on. "I also offered her some of your clothes while hers go through the dryer."

Stephanie shrugged and turned the chair around. Don't ask me to describe Stephanie's look—I can't—but warning bells clanged in my head. Offering the use of her clothes wouldn't cause such a reaction. Something else was up. "What's going on?"

Looking up, she failed to look innocent. "I was just thinking."

"About what?"

She gave me a veiled look. "The case."

I shrugged and took a seat at my desk, spinning to face her. "Really? Cause there are plenty of things you could be thinking about. One of your moods could be coming on." Her face darkened at that. "You know damn well you have them. What set it off this time? I have a list, if you need a peek."

This time her voice held more authority. "It's the case. That knife blade removed any doubt that this was preplanned. No matter how remote the chance, I wish it wasn't so. Had it been a crime of opportunity, perpetrated by an eccentric individual, then only luck has saved him thus far. But luck is a fickle mistress, and patience will eventually win out. Instead, I find myself pitted against a person who has outwitted and outmaneuvered the police and their not inconsiderable resources."

"So you're just pouting. For the record, I don't believe you. But I do have a question before you return to your brooding. If she was shot—I think we can trust the police on that one—and the murderer pried up the bullet, why leave the gun?"

"Indeed. Was the gun left in order to deceive and mislead? At this point, all we really have are a series of assumptions—assumptions our murderer wishes us to make. We must strip it all away and start fresh, only accepting that which we know to be true."

Stephanie's mouth snapped shut as the front door opened and closed. It was after hours, and no uninvited guests should be stopping in. I reached inside a lower desk drawer and pulled out the revolver I stored there, resting it on my lap. Stomping footfalls made their way to the office and I relaxed, recognizing the thumping. Detective James Hawthorne stormed in, soaked and with a face to match the thunderstorms outside.

"What the hell do you think you're doing tailing everyone tied to the Swope murder?" he roared, shoving a finger at his sister. I returned the revolver to its drawer.

"What, pray tell, are you bemoaning this time?" Stephanie's voice was as cold as ice.

"Oh, you know damn well what I'm talking about. You're involved with the Swope case now, aren't you?"

"Is there some reason I shouldn't be?"

"How about interfering with an ongoing police investigation? Is that not a good enough reason?" I thought the term *ongoing* was overkill, but I kept my trap shut.

Stephanie crossed her arms under her breasts. "Are you saying I cannot perform the duties requested by my client within the full measure the law allows without first seeking your permission?"

Answering a question with another question usually leaves people off-balance, making them defend their position. It was one of Stephanie's favorite approaches. But James knew Stephanie and her tactics from back when they shared naptime together. I'd never seen it work with him.

James's face turned purple as he got within two feet of Stephanie's desk. "Who taught you that routine? Do you really think it'll work on me?"

"I have no idea what you are referring to. Now answer my question."

And with that, the stalemate began. I sat there and watched the cycle of accusations and questions repeat itself. The constant repetition quickly got boring. I pulled out a sheet of paper and folded it.

The paper airplane sailed between the two combatants.

Both brother and sister stopped and looked at me. I returned their angry stares with a look of intense boredom. James growled something and looked back at Stephanie. "I have the chief of police breathing down my neck; he, in turn, has city hall chewing his ass because of your escapades. Some of the mayor's good friends, along with the mayor himself, have a personal interest in this case. You—"

"So, yet again, politics hinders truth and justice." All sense of composure left Stephanie's face as disgust replaced it. "At least I am here to see it done."

"Don't spout nonsense about justice. Altruism is not in your vocabulary. You're being paid, pure and simple. Where was justice when you weren't receiving a fat check?"

"So what if I am? Is it now illegal to be paid for one's services?"

I spoke up. "James. Take a seat. What's this is all about?"

James stared at me, but heaved a sigh and took a seat. "Today, word was passed down through unofficial channels that certain friends of the mayor wish to have two particular private detective licenses pulled. Yours. They don't appreciate the attention. I took it upon myself to warn you to lay off."

Stephanie's ears perked up. "Which friends?"

"I don't know all the names, but the Honorable Representative Vice was on that list." James's tone indicated his opinion of the honorific title. "As far as I could tell, we investigated every person connected to the Swope murder. These are powerful people. Do yourselves a favor and drop it."

I looked over at Stephanie as silence filled the room. It could be true, but James could also be fishing for information. And we had information to give. The knife wasn't smoking, but it sure was hot.

Leaning back in my chair, I crossed my arms. "James, I followed no one today. And you know Stephanie couldn't follow Theseus out of a shoebox." Suddenly, Stephanie's idea to use Jennifer didn't seem so foolish.

Of course, there wasn't a more inept time for Jennifer's entrance. It didn't take a genius to put two and two together, and James was smarter than his sister. His face flushed with renewed anger. Jennifer stood dumbfounded in the doorway in her borrowed clothes. Suddenly, I wished I'd heard the water shut off.

James waved angrily at Jennifer. "You dare tell me you have no idea who's tailing these people, and then you flaunt her in my face. She's your niece. I came here to help you, and you throw lies at me. At this rate, you'll be out on your ears by the end of the week."

He stomped out of the room, brushing roughly past Jennifer. I followed after him. Settling a jacket over his shoulders, he reached for the doorknob. James glared at me as I leaned against the door to keep him from leaving.

"My turn for a friendly word of advice." My voice

was barely pitched above a whisper, intended only for the two of us to hear. "Do yourself a favor—family or not—remember this is a private residence. Entering without invitation or a warrant doesn't look so good for a police detective."

His eyes flashed at me, and he yanked the door open as I stepped aside. Leaving the door wide open, he walked away. It was a petty gesture, though easily enough ignored. I shut and locked it, then returned to the office to find Stephanie watching through a window as her brother pulled away. Jennifer sat curled in a chair, nursing a glass of water. Another sat on Stephanie's desk.

Stephanie's words slid across the room, intended for no one and everyone. "Just think . . . I'm his children's godmother. It's a shame we cannot seem to see eye to eye on anything."

I took my seat, wanting my own glass of water but ignoring the need. "It would help," I said, "if you didn't antagonize one another so often. But that should be expected when the two of you are so similar." Stephanie's glare slid off me with no effect. If she didn't like the truth, then she was in the wrong profession.

"No such familial ties keep you from being removed," she said.

"Divorce? Really? That's what you're going with?

You'd be lost without me. Besides, it's my job to tell you these things, both as your husband and your employee. Where else would you find someone with my skills as chauffeur, cook, back scratch artist, and private dick?"

Jennifer snorted. Teenagers.

Stephanie turned back from the window. "He enjoys fighting. Always has. One day it was debate team, the next fistfights in the school parking lot. I've never understood why. I do wish things were different, though."

"Perhaps, but you enjoy a good fight yourself, just of a different sort. That's something I've noticed about you Hawthornes. You aren't happy unless there's a scrap brewing." I trudged over to the refrigerator, pulling out a can of something cold. Popping the top without looking, I took a hefty swallow before returning to my seat. "But we both know it takes more than wishes to change things."

Stephanie nodded. "If wishes were horses, beggars would ride."

I took another sip. "If wishes were horses, we'd all be at the races." Stephanie glanced at me and I winked back.

Jennifer spoke up. "I used to love horses as a kid. Not so much now." Preoccupied with Stephanie, I'd totally forgotten about my niece.

Stephanie knew it, too. She hid a smile behind the

rim of her glass. "Yes, well, so did I. But back to work. Report."

"Report?" Jennifer looked confused.

"Jenny, I need to know what you saw, what you did. I told you this before you left. You have to remember every detail. Work supersedes entertainment."

My mind shot back to the first night of this case, but I kept my mouth shut.

"Okay. How much do you want?"

"All of it."

Jennifer looked surprised. "All of it? But Unc doesn't tell you everything?"

"Occasionally he does, but I know your uncle and he knows me. He tells me what I need to know, and I trust him because he knows his job. You, my dear, are inexperienced and have no idea what I am looking for. So start at the beginning and be as precise as possible. Otherwise, this will be the last time I hire you to so much as mow my yard."

Jennifer sighed. There wasn't much to relate. She made it to the animal shelter around nine. Sitting under a nearby tree, she called the shelter with the sole purpose of figuring out if Helen was in her office or not. With that confirmed, Jennifer settled in for the day.

Nothing happened until 1:05 p.m. when Helen left

for a light lunch at a neighborhood deli two blocks down the street, returning to her office by 2:00. Between then and close, only three people entered: a mother and daughter pair at 3:15, leaving half an hour later with a puppy in tow, and a well-dressed man at 3:20 who left empty-handed at 4:30. At 4:40, just as the storm clouds were coming in, Helen left the animal shelter, proceeded to the bus stop, and caught the 4:45 across town, where I soon met Jennifer across from the dry cleaner's.

Stephanie raised her hand, calling for silence. "What did this man look like?"

Jennifer shrugged. "Average, I guess. Dressed fancy like a lawyer or a businessman. All suit and tie and shiny shoes."

"What did he look like physically?"

"Oh." Jennifer paused to think. "Average height, slightly heavier build, no glasses, dark brown hair. No one I've seen before."

Stephanie grunted. "Anything else?" Jennifer shook her head. "How far from the building was your tree?"

"About forty yards away or so. I didn't want to be obvious. Was that too far?"

"Yes."

Then I proceeded to evaluate the day's

performance. Stephanie let me, never interrupting once. Five minutes later, I wasn't sure Jennifer had absorbed anything, but I was tired of talking.

I turned to Stephanie. "Anything else?" She shook her head. Jennifer got the royal treatment as I escorted her out to her car, using an old umbrella to keep back the rain. She indicated that she planned to return for her clothes the next day before starting on the next round of tailing. That was fine with me. Back inside, I relocked the door and shut off the lights in the front room before returning to the office.

Stephanie still hadn't moved. I watched her for a minute or two before speaking up. "You want to hear about my day?" Taking her silence for consent, I proceeded to lay out the day's events, starting with the details from my search of the Swope house and ending with picking up Jennifer at the bus stop.

Nothing moved save for Stephanie's eyes as she looked at me. It was one of her creepier habits.   "Your thoughts? You've had more time than I to think this over. Your conclusions may be more pertinent, though that would prove a unique experience."

"It would also be unique for you to admit that I added anything to your thought processes," I said. "One gives you ten that The Suit's visit has nothing to do with

Helen's decision to pick up the dress. I don't recognize his description, and I doubt that he knew about the dress.

"But the dress is important. Did she already know about it? Did someone tell her about it? And why is it suddenly so important? That receipt proves it was undisturbed for months. What changed?"

Stephanie sighed. "We have no proof yet that it is significant. What would Mr. Wood have done with the dress after today?"

"No idea. It only survived this long because the cleaning was prepaid. He says hello, by the way."

A short-lived smile appeared on Stephanie's face before winking back out of existence. "What of the knife? Did you bring it with you?"

I shook my head. "Nope. Seemed a smarter idea to leave it right where it was. While I don't think Swope enters that room more than he has to, I think a missing knife would be noticed. If the murderer had known about the two parts, then I suspect neither the knife nor the tip would still be around."

"That knife creates quite a headache." Disgust flittered across Stephanie's face. "Enough of one that we must take steps in the morning. Call James and inform him of it after breakfast. His lackeys can busy themselves with it while we focus on more important matters."

Stephanie seemed satisfied to leave it at that. I stayed seated as she shut down the office for the night. "Is finding the owner of the phone number on that receipt going to be as easy as you believe?"

I nodded. "Should take no more than an hour."

"Good. Call Jenny after you talk to James. She can handle that. I have other tasks for you."

"Such as?"

"Helping me shut down the office for the night would be a satisfactory beginning," she said with a bit of a bite.

I acquiesced. Minutes later we were upstairs—Stephanie in the kitchen preparing dinner while I sat in the living room. She continued our previous line of discussion via the pass-through between the kitchen and the living room.

"We can keep quiet about the receipt and the heels for now. Nothing quite as conclusive indicates them as evidence in a murder. However, we skate a fine line with them. I suspect both are more important than readily apparent."

"Already proven. That receipt led to the dress," I said.

"Indeed, but the dress is not yet directly tied to the murder. I suspect it is but lack proof. Instead, it introduces its own conundrums."

"And the heels?"

Stephanie looked at me, a mix of annoyance and shock in her eyes. "That should be obvious."

"Pretend that it's not."

"Those are not Mrs. Swope's shoes." Her tone was flat, as if she was stating a fact everyone should know—which, in her mind, she was.

That didn't mean I believed her. "How do you figure?"

"Mrs. Swope, if nothing else, had huge feet for a woman. All the other shoes in the closet are three sizes larger than those heels. Look at them. They're worn out and have no place in the circles Mrs. Swope favored. So why keep them? Favorite shoes? Phooey. Nothing indicates that Mrs. Swope was a sentimental woman. I suspect it was a poor attempt to hide something in plain sight. It's a matter of importance to identity their original owner."

Wonderful smells emanated from the stove as I left my perch for the kitchen. "A bit like Cinderella, don't you think?" I heard her snort, but I ignored it and went on. "Is that what you want me to work on tomorrow?"

Stephanie shook her head. "No. That will come in time but isn't currently a priority. If it becomes one, then we'll focus on it. Instead, I want you with me. We are supposed to meet with Mrs. Vice tomorrow morning, and, even though I expect to be ignored, I want you there."

With that, the work-related conversation ceased. Stephanie talked on, but it was all mundane matters that would only bore you. If it wasn't boring, then it was personal and will not be repeated.

Chapter 11

"'Sleeping together' always seemed like an inappropriate euphuism for an activity that is anything but restful."

The next morning, I called James and passed on the information Stephanie and I had about the knife. He was more than a little upset at the news, partially because we'd held onto it for so long, but most of it was because I had upstaged his boys in lab coats. All the same, James threatened to stop by later to discuss the proper handling of potential evidence.

I gave Jennifer her new assignment when she arrived at the office, only minutes before heading off to make Stephanie's appointment. Jennifer seemed confident in getting the results, and we left her to it.

Stephanie said nothing during the drive. I wasn't surprised. I felt we'd get no further than the door; still, the attempt had to be made. Counter to my suspicions, however, we were quickly ushered inside and upstairs by a woman claiming to be Representative Vice's personal assistant. Offering us each a seat, she left us in a makeshift lobby.

We sat and were promptly ignored for the next two hours. Stephanie looked like a lump on a log as she watched everyone pass by. That seemed even worse than counting the holes in the Styrofoam tiles above our heads, which was what I had been doing. Finally, Stephanie had enough. Rudeness I knew she could bear—even if I couldn't—but total ignominy was too much. She planted herself before a passing aide. When he attempted to sidestep, Stephanie followed, blocking any forward movement.

"Where is Patricia Vice?" Stephanie's voice was ice-cold. The aide blanched amidst the storm and took a step back.

Before he could say anything, a woman, apparently senior to him, appeared. Unfazed by The Look, she stepped in front of the junior aide. With her hands neatly placed behind her back and out of Stephanie's line of sight, she waved the aid away. "Sorry for the wait. How may I help you?"

"Where. Is. Patricia. Vice?" Each word stabbed, attempting to draw blood.

"Representative Vice is currently in a meeting. She won't be available today, I'm afraid. Maybe if you come back tomorrow—"

"No." Apparently, the woman had expected polite

dissatisfaction, not a blunt refusal. Stephanie pressed her advantage. "I'll see her now."

The aide's eyes flicked to a room over Stephanie's shoulder. "As I said, she's in a meeting and can't be disturbed. I am sure she will be free—"

I didn't hear the rest. Pushing myself up, I walked toward the room the aid had indicated, ignoring the protests behind me. At Stephanie's nod, I pushed the room's door open and stepped inside, Stephanie and the aide following. The shutting door cut off all sound from the lobby.

Five people sat in overstuffed leather chairs around a rectangular table set in the middle of the room. Despite the modest origins of the building and Vice's platform, the room matched one found in any Fortune 500 company's boardroom. Wood-paneled walls highlighted art which, I felt sure, was worth more than it looked, along with a movie theater screen masquerading as a television. A tinted floor-to-ceiling window filled one wall, giving an unobstructed view to the street below. Patricia Vice sat in the middle on one side, with Jeffery Hunt on her left; every other face was that of a stranger.

Vice was the first to react to our entry. "Excuse me, this is a private meeting," she said as she scrambled to her feet.

"Indeed." Stephanie's voice was as icy as ever. "That much is apparent."

"I am sorry about this, ma'am." The voice was barely more than a squeak and came from our unintentional guide who'd entered behind us.

Vice nodded. "It's all right, Kristy. With some people, there's very little you can do." Stephanie snorted, but Vice ignored her. "I am sorry about our meeting today, Mrs. Atwell; however, this is not a good time. If you will speak with Kristy, we can reschedule." She returned to her seat.

"I think not." Stephanie opened the door. "Being snubbed once is bad enough, but I won't let it happen again. Should I speak to anyone from this point on, it will only be to newspaper reporters regarding a certain pair of red heels and a matching dress. They may find it interesting."

Vice closed her eyes and sighed as she placed her hands flat on the table. "Everyone. Out."

The room soon emptied, save for Stephanie, Patricia Vice, and myself. We took seats facing Vice. A pitcher of water and a set of crystal glasses graced the middle of the table, and I became acquainted with them. Even the water tasted expensive.

"How do you know about the dress?" Nothing

had changed about Vice, from her voice to her posture, but her body lacked the command it had displayed earlier. In fact, she seemed close to tears.

"That's of no matter. I want to know why those shoes were in Mrs. Swope's closet to begin with."

Vice met Stephanie's piercing glare. I saw a trace of backbone for a minute, and then the spirit left her altogether. "There was a fundraiser about a month before Andrea's death. One of the caterers slipped and covered me in wine. Andrea took me upstairs and was kind enough to loan me another dress. Those shoes didn't match, and I forgot them when I left that night."

"Do not spout drivel." I heard Vice's mouth slam shut at the barrage. "Not for a second do I believe that's the entire story. If you wish to maintain your position, however—" Stephanie stood as if ready to leave.

Vice blanched at the movement, her body stiffening. I poured her a glass of water and slid it across the table. She took a long gulp and continued. "The loaned dress and shoes. They were Andrea's way of telling me something. All right?"

"No. Explain."

"The dress isn't mine. It never was. Andrea pulled it from the closet, and I had no other options, so I wore it. Later, I dropped off at the dry cleaner's. I forgot about it until yesterday and sent Jeff for it." If Vice wasn't a United States Congresswoman, I'd have said she whined. Congressmen don't whine.

Stephanie grunted. "Hogwash. Yesterday was quite informative. This looks like a poor attempt to hide something. I know you will take any and all steps to prove it. This would be much less painful if you ceased the constant dodging."

At that, Vice collapsed, her ashen face buried in her hands. A sob escaped her before coherent words spurted from behind her fingers. "It was nearly a year ago now. Arthur hosted a fundraiser for me at his house. I wore the red dress there. As the night progressed, one thing led to another, and with all the alcohol involved, I drank a bit more than was wise. Andrea was out, and I ended up spending the night with Arthur. In the morning, I left in some spare clothes and forgot about the dress.

"A few months later, Andrea confronted me with it. She didn't believe Arthur about the two of us sleeping separately. She vowed to go public with it. For weeks I walked on eggshells, afraid. She said nothing until that party when she gave it back to me. It all felt planned. You know how women don't like wearing the same dress over again. She made me do it."

Stephanie snorted. "I dislike that particular

predilection. Nothing more ever came from it? Have you seen the dress since that night?"

"No." Vice let the answer stand for both questions. "I remembered it the other day and asked Jeff to handle it. He said he would, but probably forgot in this morning's rush."

"You sound as if something special occurred this morning. The action around here only supports that theory. Why the rush?"

Apparently, moving from her personal life and into politics had a soothing effect on Vice's nerves. She looked up and her voice grew stronger. "We received word early this morning through private channels that one of our opponents dropped out of the race. Not only that, but we also earned his endorsement. It took a lot of work, but he agreed to simultaneously announced his withdrawal from the race and throw his support behind me. Of course, I have to be present tonight, along with Jeff. So I would say things are a bit busy this morning."

Stephanie nodded. "What is the nature of your relationship with Mr. Swope?"

"Those rumors are *lies*!" Vice had returned to full form. A clock started in my head, ticking toward the end of the interview. "He and I share a similar political view, that's all."

"You insinuated the foundation of your relationship, but never stated it outright. As for the rumors you dismiss—I can guess. 'Sleeping together' always seemed like an inappropriate euphemism for an activity that is anything but restful. So, either you lied or I am missing information. I don't believe you took that dress to the dry cleaner's out of habit. There was something wrong with it."

"Yes." There was anger in her whispered reply. "There were . . . stains. Anyone with half a brain knew what from. She wanted to embarrass me by making me wear the same dress over again, but those stains made it worse. It was a way for her to tell everybody without expressing anything publically."

Stephanie took a sip of my water. "Since that night, Arthur's not been as supportive as you would like?"

Vice shook her head. "It didn't put him off. Only since Andrea's death has he been distant. His support—both public and private—is missed. That's why I was at his office last week. When they finally allowed me to see him, all I got was silence before being dismissed. No one likes to lose a confidant, especially in the middle of a congressional race."

"Did Mr. Swope understand the significance of the dress?"

"I should think so. Undoubtedly, only the willfully blind missed that one. I'm just glad it was a relatively minor gathering."

"Was Mrs. Swope dissatisfied with her marriage?"

Vice stood. "You'll have to ask Arthur. I have no more time today, Mrs. Atwell. There are other matters which require my attention. Good day." She left, shutting the door firmly behind her.

"It's Hawthorne," I said. The room took no notice.

Stephanie stayed seated, facing the window. I refilled my glass and took a sip as I counted the seconds in my head. When I reached three hundred, I spoke up.

"The Tigers won last night." I leaned back in my chair and crossed my legs. "I thought they'd lost it in the sixth."

That had the intended effect. Stephanie frowned at me and walked around the table to stand before the window. "I dislike politicians."

"Lying comes with the territory."

"No. Politics just hones those skills. Lying is not the first line of defense for politicians. Nothing beyond public opinion determines whether or not politicians disguise their views."

Stephanie refused to say more as we left the

meeting room and the top floor behind. Reaching the car took only a minute more, and we were on our way back to the office.

Stephanie looked at me from the corner of her eye. I didn't actually see it, but I knew it was there. "What did James say this morning?"

I told her, leaving out the expletives and the idle threats. She knew they were there all the same.

"Do we have enough time to stop at the police station?"

"No dice." The station was the other direction, and we were late as it was. "Unless you gave Jennifer a key and didn't tell me. I'm not a fan of my niece sitting outside in this heat just because you want to go another round with your brother."

"Discussing the knife is hardly a frivolous matter."

"I agree. It's not frivolous. But we both know that as soon as he finishes, he'll seek us out to question everything we said. Since we lie so much. There's no reason to believe he will act different this time. What you're doing is avoiding Helen Black."

"Mrs. Swope."

"Don't start that with me. You're just being peevish. Of all people, you have no ground to stand on in regard to married women giving up their maiden names. She's Helen Black. Accept it. If I have to, you do as well.

"What you're doing is avoiding her. All roads lead to Rome. In this case, *she's* Rome. What ties her to Hunt? What about Vice? Why did she pick up the dress when Hunt was sent for it?"

"I have not been avoiding her." The woman could be so damn stubborn.

I couldn't hold it in any longer and let out a bellowing laugh. "Yes, you have. Last time you went in cocky and got singed. You never finished that conversation because of it."

Stephanie insisted on the police station. I just ignored it.

Chapter 12

"Not many men can resist a beautiful young woman trying to reconnect with her estranged father. But a low-cut top didn't hurt my case either."

We found Jennifer by the garage, reading some book or another. With the greetings soon finished, the stifling heat drove us all inside. As I walked down the hallway toward the office, I could see through the window in the front door to the grass outside. Something about it called to me, and I went over to look.

Nothing appeared out of the ordinary at first glance. I unlocked the door and stepped outside. The grass needed to be cut, but my schedule had yet to allow me the opportunity. Just as well, otherwise I would have missed the wide circle trampled by the door. I bent over to examine it and almost missed the glint of a key on its own ring hidden under a tuft of grass next to the sidewalk. Picking it up, my eyes made contact with the door itself. Fresh scrapes twisted around the keyhole and the door frame. I pulled out my own key and tested the lock before heading back inside.

I took a seat at my desk. "Well, someone didn't like that we were closed this morning." Stephanie and Jennifer, already occupying the same seats as the night before, looked up at me.

"What are you talking about?" Stephanie sounded disgusted, but that changed as I told her about the grass, the key, and the door. When I finished, she picked up the phone and punched in the numbers from memory. Two minutes later, Stephanie had her brother on the other end of the line.

The conversation started out quite civilly and, I admit, remained so longer than I expected, but soon family history won out, and it degraded into a sibling shouting match. It ended abruptly as Stephanie stopped talking and looked at the handset.

"He hung up. That rotten little twerp hung up on me."

I chuckled under my breath. Or maybe I laughed out loud, because Stephanie glared at me and my niece looked shocked.

"Are you surprised? Especially after the knife? Let me guess. He accused you of crying wolf, seeking attention, and hiding information relevant to his investigation. Also, there was the obligatory bit about getting our licenses pulled. You know James. It's the same old song and dance. He needs to find a new line."

Stephanie nodded. "Quite, but I expected him to show more concern about a possible break-in at his sister's house."

"You heard him. You're just clamoring for attention. He won't believe you until the next time he visits and then only if his rage doesn't blind him to it."

Stephanie sighed and pinched the bridge of her nose. "Jenny, did you have any luck with that number?"

Jennifer nodded. "I expected it to be a cell phone; most numbers seem to be these days. This one wasn't, though. At first, all I found out was that it's registered somewhere in the city. To find out where would have cost me, and I didn't want to pay." She shrugged. "Instead, I went to the phone company and wheedled it out of a nice gentleman there."

"Wheedled it out how?" I raised an eyebrow, disapproval in my voice.

"Not many men can resist a beautiful young woman trying to reconnect with her estranged father." Jennifer leaned forward and pressed her breasts together with her arms. "But a low-cut top didn't hurt my case either."

I closed my eyes and shook my head. This was not something an uncle wanted to know about his niece. It was then that Stephanie's low chuckle drifted my way from across the room.

Maybe I glared at Stephanie, but I won't admit it—which only made her laugh harder. "How do you think our niece performed?" Returning her attention to Jennifer, Stephanie went on. "It's been years since I had to pull that trick. We may make a detective out of you yet. What's the address?"

It was tied to an apartment building on East Jefferson in one of the working-class neighborhoods. That was of little immediate help. The address Jennifer found lacked the apartment number, and a return to the phone company was pressing our luck.

Stephanie sat in silence, eyes closed and hands steepled in front of her. Best to leave her to decide on our next move. My stomach rumbled, and Jennifer looked at me in amusement. I gathered her up with a look and walked out the door, leaving Stephanie where she sat. Fifteen minutes later, Stephanie joined us just as I finished off the cold fried chicken. Stephanie reheated some of the leftovers from last night's dinner and settled down at the table with Jennifer and me.

"What's the next step?" I asked.

"I require a list of tenants from the apartment complex."

"Won't happen," Jennifer said around a mouthful of leftovers. "I thought a list would help, so I tried to find one after I finished at the phone company. There's no supervisor, no office manager, no office to speak of. If you want a list, you'll have to make it up yourself."

"You should have mentioned this before." Stephanie remained impassive, but both of us could read between the lines. "Jennifer, I want you to go back to that building and watch it like a hawk. You can take my car. Notify us if you recognize anyone coming or going. I'll send someone to relieve you later."

I fished out a spare set of car keys from a drawer in the kitchen and handed them to Jennifer. Despite the ease of the job, I cautioned her to take care of the vehicle and to keep a sharp eye out. She nodded and left.

Once we finished eating, Stephanie and I went back downstairs to the office. Taking a seat at my desk, I propped my feet up on a corner. "You have someone in mind to help her watch that building?"

Stephanie had placed a glass of water on her blotter before settling at her desk. Now she took a sip and peered at me over the rim. I nodded, dropped my feet, and dialed Logan Ambrose. Logan was as good a PI as you could get in this town. A solid professional and a good friend. It only took a minute to sketch the details for him.

"Logan will relieve Jennifer at eleven tonight. He suggests we set up twelve-hour rotations for now, but if it goes on too long, we should add a third person. I agree."

Stephanie grunted. I called Jennifer and explained the set-up. When the line went dead for a second time in ten minutes, I got a nod of approval and that's it.

Unfortunately, this left me with a slight problem. My head said "go, run, look," but my gut told me to stay put. I wanted to be out there, looking for something, anything—from who owned that phone number to discovering the connection between Helen Black and Jeffery Hunt. Yet I dared not. Stephanie had something specific she wanted to do, but I had no clue what it was.

I looked over at my wife. She sat back in her chair, eyes closed and fingers occasionally twitching. The sun cast yellow swaths of light through the window and across the garishly-colored sweater of blue, orange, and pink she wore thanks to my absolute control over the thermostat. Holding my peace took some work, but I succeeded. Stephanie opened her eyes and picked up the phone. Despite the distance, I could hear the tones as she hit each number.

"Is Mr. Jeffery Hunt available? I wish to speak to him."

I wasn't sure what she was doing. Not three hours

before, we'd been at the campaign headquarters. Stephanie could've talked to Hunt then but had chosen not to do so. Why now?

Catching Stephanie's eye, I raised an inquisitive brow. She took pity on me, placed the phone on speaker, and cradled the handset. A minute later, a voice I recognized came on the line. "This is Jeffery Hunt. How may I help you?"

"Mr. Hunt, this is Stephanie Hawthorne. Do you have a minute?"

His sigh echoed through the speaker. "I'm afraid not. It's been a hectic day, and it's going to be an even longer night."

"I can appreciate that." Stephanie picked up a pen and scribbled a note on a scrap of paper. "I was wondering if you would call on me at my office tonight. What I wish to talk about may take some time, and privacy might be important to you. I'm not sure how private we'd be at the campaign headquarters."

"I'm afraid that's impossible. Things are moving fast here, and I won't be free for a while. Maybe we could talk in a few days."

"Unfortunately, that won't work." Stephanie stood and handed me the note. She returned to her desk and picked up the handset, returning the call to its normal settings. I listened in as best I could as I followed her instructions. "I must have the answer to one or two things. The rest can wait. I'll send Mr. Atwell over. Expect him by three." Pausing, she listened. "Satisfactory. Good day."

I caught the last of the conversation as I dug out the phone number for Swope Law offices. My call stalled when Miss Swanson answered the phone, apparently still on switchboard duty. She blocked my efforts for fifteen minutes, and it took a couple lies and a promise before she put me through to Robert Swope. It only took a matter of seconds to convince him to visit Stephanie at the office.

Hanging up, I turned to Stephanie. "All done. He'll be here by four-thirty. A bit later than you wanted, but that saves me from rushing back here after meeting with Hunt."

Stephanie had taken up her book and now spoke without looking up. "You'll miss the meeting—or at least most of it. I need you to run an errand."

This failed to please me in the least.

Chapter 13

"What do you want first?"
"Nothing. I want nothing to do with this case."

In all the time I've known Stephanie, she has never once played games. I don't know why. I've heard rumors of a game of Go Fish which resulted in a broken nose and a black eye. Perhaps because of this, she avoids anything related to games, including common jargon. Not once has she used terms like "home run" or "no dice" in my presence, despite their inclusion in my vocabulary.

Perhaps that is why, when I called her out on our lack of progress a week later, she referred to our activities as a "constructive gambit based on conclusions made during the course of the investigation, intended to create instability and doubt." Eighteen words to avoid two. A bluff. We were playing Blind Man's Bluff. Marco Polo. Tag. Sometimes I don't understand that woman.

Even though it took me a week to confirm, my first hint at her intentions appeared as I left to meet with Hunt. Despite Hunt's claim of being too busy to leave, the offices were mostly abandoned. A lone janitor roamed the too-quiet halls. With half the lights off, the once cheerful place now took on an eerie cast.

Hunt's office was the only completely lit room. He stood before his desk, his briefcase spread open before him. I knocked on the doorframe. The only response it elicited was a glance in my direction before he continued with his packing, shoving his briefcase full of files from three separate cabinets.

"I heard about your performance earlier. I'm not sure I want to talk to you after that. I don't like dealing with people who lack the understanding of propriety."

I took a seat across from his desk. "You misheard. That wasn't me. We kept our appointment. Besides, propriety requires conformity to the established standards of good manners, which were lacking at the time. So, how about we not have that conversation?"

He glanced over his shoulder at me and shrugged. "As you wish. What was so important that your boss refused to leave us alone?"

"She wanted to know your impressions of Robert and Helen Swope."

"Is that it?"

"As far as I know, yes."

He shook his head. "Robert came to only a few functions. He's a minor donor in his own right, but that might have more to do with his father than any actual political interest. As for Helen, keeping her maiden name drove the Swopes nuts. It was a frequent topic of conversation. She came to even fewer events than Robert. Every time, she tried to drum up support for that charity of hers. Occasionally, it would even work."

I balanced one shoe upon the other. "She seemed to be quite a character when we met. Unfortunately, she left such an unfavorable impression on Mrs. Hawthorne that she refuses to talk to her. I'm in a real pickle here."

Hunt had finished packing his overstuffed briefcase. "What do you want me to do about it? Sounds like a personal problem."

"Understand that this is from me, not Mrs. Hawthorne. I want to ask a favor of you. Can you speak to Helen? Convince her to talk to us? No gimmicks. Scout's honor." I raised three fingers.

I didn't care what Hunt said. It was his reaction I was interested in. His voice held strong as he grabbed his briefcase, but his face . . . . Poker obviously wasn't his game of choice. "You misunderstand me. I have no interest in seeing you or Mrs. Hawthorne succeed. The police will handle it. Now, I must insist you leave. This conversation is over, and I'm late as it is."

I followed him out without another word. We

stood on the curb outside the building before he spoke again.

"Maybe, if I happen to see her, I might remember to mention it. Maybe not. Don't count on it. I don't see her very often. For obvious reasons." He indicated one of Vice's campaign signs sitting in the corner.

I nodded, and he walked around the corner and out of sight. Stage one complete, I jogged across the street to my car. From where it was parked, I not only had a good view of the two corner streets, but I also had an angled view of the side street and Hunt. Moments later, Hunt's car pulled out and headed east.

He drove aggressively. I don't think he was trying to lose a tail, but rather drove the way one does when late and trying to make up time. Half an hour later, I pulled to a stop in the center of town and within an easy walk of city hall. Hunt emerged from a nearby parking garage and sprinted to the governmental building.

I dodged traffic and jogged across the street to the building Hunt had entered. There was a sign taped to the front door advertising a rally with Patricia Vice. I glanced at my watch. The event was set to start in five minutes. I declined the invitation and returned to my car. This rally wasn't for me, and its legitimacy could be checked easily enough. The engine turned over, and I pulled out.

I meandered in a southwestern direction, not
rushing to reach my destination. Hunger gnawed at me,
and I thought about my next destination before stopping
at a kosher deli for a couple sandwiches. Back in the car, I
pulled the pickle from the second one. That was mine. Call
it the cost of doing business. Finishing my meal took no
time at all, and I soon drove off to find my wife's car.

It sat parked in front of a massive maple tree.
Circling the block, I found a place to park down the street.
I got out, making sure to grab the sandwich, and strolled
toward the parked car. As I walked, I took a moment to
study the building we had under surveillance. It was an
eight-story concrete and marble monolith, snuggled up
between a five-story red-brick tenement on its right and a
seven-story office building on its left. Judging from the
architecture, it was probably built in the fifties but looked
to be doing well for its age. Built in a nondescript gray,
there wasn't a single thing that stood out about it. It was,
simply put, boring.

Reaching the passenger door, I knocked on the
window, waved, and heard the door unlock in response. I
slid into the car and handed her the roast beast on rye. She
thanked me as I adjusted myself in the seat.

"Go stretch your legs," I said. "Get a drink, use
the bathroom, whatever you need to do. Be back in fifteen

minutes." Jennifer nodded, sandwich in hand, and bolted from the car. From the way she moved, I had guessed right about the whole bathroom situation. I banished her from my mind and focused on the building.

Stephanie filled the silence in my head, and I wondered—unintentionally—about her meeting with Robert Swope. My orders were completed easily enough, but I'd been banned from the office, so all I could do was speculate. And speculate I did.

Jennifer came back to the car twenty minutes later. I chided her on that, expecting promptness and trying to instill the need for an accurate internal clock or, failing that, a good watch. She accepted it in silence. Receiving none of the retort I expected, I changed the subject and asked for a report.

No one had entered the building since Jennifer had arrived earlier. I sighed. This might go on for a while. Telling her when to expect Logan and when to relieve him took only the space of a minute or two. The rest of the two hours I spent in the car, I resumed the role of teacher. Discussing techniques and other aspects of detective work ate up the time, but I was there for one other reason: companionship is important on your first stakeout.

Hours later, I stepped out onto the curb. It hadn't taken much to elicit a promise to relieve Logan on time. I guess she didn't need to promise, but I asked for it all the same. No hesitation. That was good. Intending to wish her luck, I turned back to the car but kept quiet instead. She sat with her eyes glued on the building, her mouth stuffed with the remains of pastrami on rye. It was quite a sight, and one I particularly didn't want to disturb. I returned to my car.

I could've made it home in no time, but I had things on my mind. Despite Stephanie's and my recent actions, I wasn't sold on Jennifer joining the trade. Jennifer was a bright girl, the type who made medical school seem a breeze or compared molecular chemistry to Legos. I had a hard enough time with actual Legos. This life was fine for me. I had chosen it, but I lacked the talent she had. There was so much more in life for Jennifer to experience before becoming jaded like Stephanie and me. But I lacked any peace of mind on the matter by the time I pulled out of my reverie and into the garage. All things would settle in time. Until then, we had whiskey.

But as I walked into the office, all thoughts of a drink left my mind. Stephanie still sat in her chair. That much was expected. What I didn't anticipate was Robert Swope, who jumped up at my unexpected entrance. I nodded to him, noticing the set of his jaw and the sheen of sweat on his forehead as I stood in the doorway. Wringing his hands, Robert returned to his seat at my nod.

Robert's apparent need for my consent would irritate Stephanie to no end, but I had my own considerations. Nervous interviewees seldom lead to conducive, let alone coherent, conversations. Stephanie had forgotten this little tidbit. I walked out of the room. No one said anything as I left, but Robert turned to watch me go.

I returned a minute later, glass of ice water in my hand, and handed it to Robert. He mumbled something I took for gratitude and sipped. Three swallows later, he finished the glass. Refilling it took a moment. This time it took seven sips for the glass to sit nearly empty on a nearby table.

Stephanie spoke as I took a seat behind my desk and crossed my legs. "I believe you were describing your relations with the Vice campaign, Mr. Swope." It was a statement, not a question.

"Yes." Robert cleared his throat. "Yes, I suppose I was. Um . . . I never had much to do with the campaign or its organizers. Father would inform me when he expected my appearance. That was seldom more than a day before the event. Of course, that's all stopped now."

"What is Mrs. Swope's opinion on these events?"

"Helen seems to enjoy them, but I'm not sure. She

always seems to know everything about my life, but I seldom understand hers. Whenever I passed on Father's demands to Helen, she never said anything. But she always went."

Stephanie grunted. "What do you remember of the last event your father hosted?"

Robert paused a moment to finish off his glass of water. He spoke around crunching ice. "Well, it was at his house. That wasn't typical, but it wasn't unheard of. Mom might have forced Father to hold it there. I . . . I don't know. That would've been unusual. She kept out of Father's affairs. I knew nothing about it until the day of the party. I don't remember much, other than the whole waiter incident."

"Waiter incident?"

"Some time that night, a waiter slipped and spilled wine all down Representative Vice's dress. Mother loaned one of her dresses to Vice for the rest of the night. Other than that, nothing much happened."

"Anyone notice how the waiter slipped?"

"Not me." Robert shrugged. "I'd had a bit too much to drink by then, and what I do remember comes in bits and pieces. But afterward, I did see Mom and Representative Vice in some sort of hushed conversation. No idea what was said, but the next thing I knew,

Representative Vice had changed dresses. Nothing beyond that and the rumor. "

Stephanie's lips pinched and her brow furrowed. "Mr. Swope, you try me. What rumor are you speaking of?"

Robert shrunk down in the chair. "A few days later, I heard some of the guests saying that Mom tripped the waiter to purposely spill the wine on Representative Vice. But as I said, that's nonsense. Mom wouldn't have done that—at least not without drinking much more than she had that night. I know that one for sure."

"Did your wife leave with you that night?"

Raising the glass to his lips again, he repeated his earlier actions with the ice. "No. Earlier, she'd wanted me to meet some people interested in her work. I declined, but Helen spent the night talking with them. When I left, they were still talking. She said she would get a ride home either that night or in the morning."

"Indeed." Stephanie stood and walked to door. "Oh, one more question." She made it seem like the afterthought it wasn't. "Did you see your wife again that night?"

Robert shook his head. "I didn't see her again until late the next night. We were both busy."

"Thank you for your time, Mr. Swope. I'll

consider what you said." She left the room, Robert's eyes on her back. Or on her backside. I couldn't quite tell which.

Ushering Robert out of the office took no time at all. His stride indicated he wanted to leave just as much as I wanted him to go. Out of sheer politeness, I held the car door as he climbed in. But I couldn't let him go just yet. I still had one more question to ask. Something for myself. "I have to ask. What did the dress look like? You know, the one Representative Vice changed into."

Robert thought a moment and then described it but wanted to know why. I nodded as sagely as I could. It probably made me look more like a cartoon character from the 1960s than anything else. "Fact checking. All part of the job." Robert looked puzzled but drove off without another word.

Locking the doors behind me, I shut down the front room before returning to the office. Stephanie had returned to her desk, but in the intervening minutes had found time to make some popcorn. A bowl of it sat in her lap. Silently vowing to drink more water, and discarding my earlier desire for a drink, I fetched a Pepsi out of the refrigerator.

I broke the silence. "What do you want first?"

"Nothing. I want nothing to do with this case, but

I must. Summarize it."

I did so, briefly describing everything from my conversation with Hunt to seeing Robert off. She said nothing, just sat there eating that damn popcorn. "Enough of me," I said. "I thought you intended to finish your conversation with Robert before I got home."

Stephanie lifted a kernel to her mouth. She always ate them one at a time. I could never manage that. "Correct, except the conversation was more like pulling teeth than anything useful."

"Well, I learned something useful. Actually, two somethings." Stephanie gestured for me to get on with it. "Robert just confirmed that Vice actually wore the red dress at the party. For what it's worth, I believe him. He vaguely remembered seeing it before then but was unsure as to where or when. A bit of searching about and I am sure we'll figure that out."

Stephanie nodded. "So I already assumed; however, the confirmation is welcome."

"Thank you. Also, Hunt did not pick up Helen at the dry cleaner's. His trip today proves it, and I doubt he owns more than one vehicle after seeing what he drives. We can prove that later, if you like. That being said, the car that did pick up Ms. Black was readily available had you seen your guest out. Of course, the pursuit of popcorn is an honorable venture."

Stephanie leaned back in her chair. "It matched in all aspects?" I agreed that it had. She put the nearly empty bowl of popcorn on the desk. "Anything else?"

I shook my head. "Not that I can think of." And that was that. The bowl of popcorn was still there the next morning.

Chapter 14

"Last week, there was this knife—"

That was the last tangible progress we made over the next three weeks. Everything shifted into waiting mode, and as much as I hated it, there wasn't much else to do.

I passed the time as best as I could. Unfortunately, that still left me with more hours to fill than is reasonably feasible. Stephanie claimed she could find more work for me, but we both knew it wasn't what I was looking for. Besides, I had been neglecting the upkeep on both the building and the business. Both were trumped by Stephanie's honey-do list. I rebelled on occasion by suggesting new avenues to pursue, none of which Stephanie appreciated. For her, the case now centered around the apartment—to the exclusion of everything else.

For example, two days after we learned about Robert Swope's car, I suggested that I follow him for kicks. A little extra paranoia wouldn't hurt anything. The next day, I suggested we attempt to locate Mrs. Swope's real jewelry. Three days after that, I changed the suggested tail from Robert Swope to Patricia Vice or Jeffery Hunt. I even risked suggesting a meeting with Helen Black.

Each attempt was rebuffed, with the only difference being the manner of its execution. Tailing Vice or Hunt met scorn, while a suggestion that we talk to James found feigned shock and hurt. Bring up Helen and Stephanie simply left the room without a word.

I concede that most of these suggestions were long shots, but I preferred that to pacing restlessly. More than once I found some thin excuse to leave the office and Stephanie behind. Don't get me wrong, I love my wife, but there are times when she drives me crazy. Though, I'm sure that I do the same to her at times.

Stephanie recognized the signs and left me alone, for the most part. There was little to stop me from leaving the office for hours on end with nothing more than an estimated return time. Yet, I still spent the majority of those days sitting at my desk, distracted and only pretending to work.

That isn't to say I had nothing to do regarding the case. The same day I suggested following Robert Swope around, Stephanie instructed me to hire another person to assist with watching the apartment building. Our third man turned out to be Logan's cousin through marriage, a guy by the name of John Hastings. He had similar aspirations as Jennifer but lacked the temperament. Logan wasn't too fond of him and figured this would bore him out of the business. I agreed to play along. You don't need to be a rocket scientist to watch a building, so John took over the night shift, relieving Jennifer at eight in the evening.

While the time slot was purely by chance, it turned out to be fortuitous for Jennifer. Apparently John believed himself a ladies' man and took every opportunity to share this opinion with the fairer sex. Jennifer wanted no part of it; she was much more interested in the job at hand. But since he started after her, it was up to Jennifer how much she wanted to listen to. When I learned of his behavior, I shared what Logan had told me about his cousin.

That being said, I relieved Jennifer early when I could, allowing her to have a semblance of a social life. Most of the time she took me up on the offer, but other times we would sit there discussing everything from friends to boys to rumors. It was all very gossipy.

Whenever she could, Jennifer would turn the discussion to detective work. I didn't always let it go there; there would be plenty of time for that later. But whenever I did, she listened with rapt attention, absorbing every detail and tidbit from my years of exposing others' secrets. Her ability to recall these scraps shocked me on more than one occasion. I don't know why, though. Jennifer was a bright girl.

My occasional updates from Logan revealed that Jennifer had similar conversations with him. As often as she could, Jennifer convinced Logan to spend a few extra minutes discussing a technique or clarifying some point from our discussions. Each detective has his—or her—own unique trade secrets. Sharing doesn't come easy, even with a few too many drinks, so Jennifer's conversations put me on edge. Yet she was eager to learn, and she could do much worse for a teacher. Privately, I hoped Logan would scare her away from becoming a private detective.

Stephanie was perhaps the least productive of all of us. Despite everyone else's attentions, she finished countless books, cooked thirteen meals, taught three classes, and on one occasion, attended a movie marathon put on by one of her few friends. That was an all-day affair which resulted in her drunkenly singing show tunes when she returned well after dark.

As a direct result of that night, and expressly against Stephanie's wishes, I decided to visit James at the police station the next day. Two weeks had passed, and I was sick of waiting. I knew I was opening a can of worms, but even James's condescension would be a nice change of pace from Stephanie's apathy.

James's office was stereotypical for any man proficient in his profession. A table stacked with papers sat against one wall and was flanked by bookcases, each filled to overflowing with tomes that I'm sure had something to do with his occupation. His desk was solid wood, the top worn smooth from decades of elbows. A blotter filled with notes and dates sat under a keyboard connected to the outdated computer next to the desk. Behind him, an oversized printer, a common model from ten years ago, sat on a third table barely large enough to hold it. Light streamed in from two windows, illuminating particles of dust which floated about like will-o'-the-wisps. The only non-regulation items were the two pictures of his kids on the wall, their photographs a good five years out of date.

Asking about my nephews brought a scowl to James's face. "As well as they can be with a father gone more often than not," he said, taking a sip of coffee. Past practice told me it was probably cold. "I doubt you're here to ask about my kids."

I refrained from any quips I could have made. You should be proud of me. "For the record, Stephanie and I do care how they're doing. It's just you I have problems with." James's eyes narrowed. One step forward, two steps back.

"You're lucky you're family. Anyone else talk to

me that way, they spend a night in the drunk tank. Sobriety not withstanding."

"I'll make sure to thank Stephanie."

The scowl deepened. "She could benefit from a night there herself. I don't care if you tell her that either."

I never would. "I wanted to ask you about that knife. Any leads from it?"

James's lips parted in a toothy smile as he leaned back in his chair. "Stumped, are we? The great detectives need some help?" He grunted. That was a family trait. "Why should I tell you a damn thing?"

I gave myself a ten-count. "Who said we're stumped? And besides, *you* were stumped and we helped you out. I figured a little quid pro quo was in order."

His smirk broadened into an outright grin. I could see the pieces clicking into place behind his bloodshot eyes. "Steph has no idea you're here, does she?" He held up his hand. "No need to answer. She'd never consent to my assistance in anything unless desperation had set in. And it hasn't, otherwise she would be here herself. Oh, this makes it all the sweeter." He chuckled.

My voice was cold. "I told you we are pursuing our own leads, separate from any you may consider. Now if you're done, either help or hinder. If the former, I'll stay and attempt not to take too much of your time. If the latter, you know where to find me when you change your mind."

It just made him laugh all the harder. Which annoyed me to no end. This felt more and more like a bad idea. If he kicked me out then and there, we weren't any worse off. If he should tell Stephanie, there was little I could do about it. I'd just have to take my lumps.

"A bit aggressive for someone asking for help, don't you think? You come to my job, ask for my help, and then have the audacity to insult me? I tell you what. You give me something, and I'll think about sharing.

"No dice. Do you expect us to do your job for you? It's tit for tat, James, not Christmas. We did our part, now pay the piper."

James pulled an unlabeled folder from a desk drawer. He leafed through it for a minute, selected a page, and plucked it out from the rest. He glanced at it as he spoke, double-checking the information. "Prior to your phone call, we weren't aware of either the broken knife or the location of its missing tip. I gave the boys in lab coats an earful for missing that one. However, once we had both, we were able to confirm that the two pieces were once part of the same object. That seemed the case, but confirmation was nice.

"Nothing unusual on the handle. It was covered in

fingerprints, with each member of the Swope family represented. That includes Robert and Helen. But it would be appreciated if you could keep yours off next time. All in all, the knife doesn't answer anything. In fact, it provides more questions than answers."

That interested me. "Such as?"

James took a sip of coffee. "We have a body, complete with murder weapon and bullet hole. There are matching holes through the mattress and bedsprings that, when aligned with the body, indicate that the bullet went through the body, through the bed, and into the floor. Yet we have no bullet. It should have impacted and stuck. Instead, the floor indicates a ricochet with no indication of secondary impacts.

"Now add in your knife and, despite the obvious signs, it's clear that the bullet was dug out, breaking the knife in the process. So where is the bullet? The murderer could have taken off with it, afraid we could use it to identify him. But that's just bad Hollywood science. So why take it? Common sense dictates the opposite: leave the bullet and take the gun. But that isn't what happened. I want to know why."

It was a good question, one to which I had no immediate answer. "Nothing unusual about the prints on the knife?"

"Nope. I have alibis for every print you didn't wipe away. Everyone—and I do mean everyone—has plausible deniability. Hell, even Representative Vice gave me a reasonable explanation for her prints. Arthur Swope backed her up. There's really nothing to go on. Either the killer knew fingerprints weren't going to be a problem or, more likely, he wore gloves."

"That it?"

James nodded. "Unfortunately so. Not much of an improvement, is it?"

I cursed under my breath. "Thanks for the help. We'll be in touch." I started for the door.

"Hey!" James jumped to his feet. "What are you doing? You still owe me. Sit down and spill." He pointed to my recently vacated chair.

Pursing my lips, I pretended to give it some thought. "Last week, I was at Arthur Swope's house and there was this knife—"

"Beat it, jackass."

I illustrated that it is best not to argue with a police detective.

Telling Stephanie my whereabouts earned me a scowl and a diatribe which was more annoying than anything else. I walked out on her. She and I both knew that her brother's information was important. But later that day, Stephanie remained at her desk, staring off into space. Obviously something had sparked in her brain. After waiting for a bit, I wandered off to catch up on the yard work that was long overdue.

As I stood in the garage, I checked my pockets and fished out the key I'd found by the front stoop. I'd stuck it in my pocket to ask James to look into it, but held off. There was no guarantee it was connected to the murder, so it stayed put. Now I examined it for the ten millionth time. It was nothing special, a typical house key, bronze in color and slightly worn. No numbers were stamped on either side, with only the embossed name of the manufacturer still visible. Slipping it onto an old key ring I pulled from one of my workbench drawers, I attached it to my personal set of keys. If I was right and the key was related to this case, I wanted it with me for the foreseeable future.

Chapter 15

"No rush. Don't think she's going anywhere."

And now you know the entire list of highlights for those three weeks. My hopes that our investigation wouldn't stall disappeared with my visit to James. The police had hit a wall. Again. Despite our efforts, Andrea's killer still refused to give himself away, leaving us to watch a building on the off-chance that we might recognize someone. Patricia Vice continued on the campaign trail, Hunt at her heels. The Swopes—both father and son— kept working on their respective cases. Jennifer, Logan, and his cousin continued their surveillance on the apartment building day in and day out with nothing even resembling a nibble. I assumed Helen Black still managed her shelter. Stephanie focused on her reading and knitting.

This left me twisting in the wind and pondering one particular question. Two weeks after it started eating at my mind, I finally asked it aloud. Why had Andrea Swope been murdered? The problem was, I had nothing to go on. Motives are as varied as people. They aren't as easy to determine as television would have us believe. But if you dig deep enough, you will find common threads: greed, power, sex.

A week after my visit with James, I'd had enough. I found Stephanie sitting on our couch that afternoon reading yet another romance. She went through those things like candy. Moving her legs, I took a seat underneath them. She looked up from her book at the intrusion.

I slid down and put my feet up on the coffee table, earning a frown. "Got a question for you. Why was Andrea killed?"

Stephanie closed her book and laid it inches from my feet. "That's the question. I'm not sure, though I do have one or two ideas. At this point, we've had more success ruling out reasons than selecting a particular one as correct."

"Stephanie, I'm serious."

"So am I. Certain motivations—money, politics, the like—can be ruled out. This murder was executed with premeditation and forethought, but it reeks of being personal. Therefore, we must question if that day was mere convenience or if her wedding anniversary held particular symbolism."

I held up a hand. "Wait. Explain it again, but this time as if I were five."

Stephanie shook her head. "Remember, Andrea had no way to support herself. She lacked a trade, skills, and anything beyond the ability to be noticed. Everything came from others. The charity work was blatantly public, and I suspect Mr. Swope was not extravagant in his attentions. Look at her jewelry, almost all of it paste. If she had better, where was it? Also, consider a simple fact: It's hard to extort money from a dead body.

"If her murder were political, it would have been symbolic. Any symbolism which resulted from her death was too obscure for the masses to prove worthwhile. That means, if her death was a warning, it was personal, designed to target one or two particular people. Her only true political ties came through the animal shelter or via her husband's relationship with Mrs. Vice.

"Since Mrs. Swope's death has had little effect on the Vice campaign, aside from Mr. Swope's departure, I doubt politics served as the motivation. We saw that during both of our visits to their campaign headquarters. That doesn't mean there wasn't any personal impact. We all know there was. Could that be important? Possibly, but I am unsure as to what extent.

"As for the animal shelter, that is a much greater mystery. What about Mrs. Swope's self-destructive nature allowed her to consistently return to that one entity? I

suspect only she and Mrs. Helen Black know the truth."
Stephanie shot a glare at me as she used the name.
"Whatever it was, I am just as positive that Ms. Black will
refuse to discuss the situation. That is the reason I have
not tried to contact her, despite what you may think."

I opened my mouth to rejoin, but the phone rang.
Stephanie made no move to answer it and reached for her
book instead. With a disgruntled shove, I extracted myself
from beneath her legs and managed to answer it on the
fourth ring. Jennifer, excitable as a puppy being fed,
shouted something unintelligible into my ear.

"Slow down." Stephanie looked up at my tone,
but I ignored her. "Now, tell me what's going on."
Jennifer's words still came at me as if they were trying to
outrun one another.

When she paused for a breath, I cut her off. "Are
you still in front of the building?"

"No. My phone died, and I had to run down to a
drugstore to call."

"Okay." Not what I wanted to hear. "Go back. I'll
be there in a minute. Wait for me. Now go!"

I hung up and turned to Stephanie. "Seems you
may have a chance to speak with Mrs. Black sooner than
you wanted. She just entered the apartment building. You
heard the conversation. Instructions?"

Stephanie's annoyance was palpable and she grimaced. "Bring her here."

Excitement at a break in the case made the trip seem both quick and endless. The power of perception. Jennifer stood in a doorway as I pulled up across from the apartment building. By the time I got out of the car, she was beside me.

"Anything change?" She shook her head and we crossed the street. I stopped her at the door. "Stay here. I need to know if anyone leaves. Don't approach them; just watch."

"Like hell." Jennifer had a glint in her eye that I recognized all too well. I didn't want her along, but I had no time for an argument. And odds were that it would take more than words to stop her from following. My niece beamed as I held the door for her.

I made a beeline for the stairs as I entered, ignoring the elevator. Jennifer never complained as I raced up the stairs two at a time. On each landing, I paused long enough to open the door to the floor and scan for abnormalities before moving on to the next. Jennifer double-checked behind me but never spoke up.

On the next-to-last floor, I stopped as something drew me into the hallway. Nothing seemed out of the ordinary at first, but my gut told me something was off.

Then I saw the elevator indicator: someone was headed down. I ordered Jennifer back down the stairs. I wanted to know who was on their way out. She didn't argue with me, and shot back down the stairs at a breakneck pace.

I glanced about as I crossed into the hallway. Nothing particularly distinctive stood out. A beige carpet with red edging covered the floor. An uneven coat of industrial-white paint was slapped on the walls. Other than the elevator, its stainless steel doors marred by scratches and dings, four other doors, each marked with the floor number and a corresponding letter, created the only exits from the hallway. Everything else—from the lighting to the carpet stains—seemed standard for a building of this sort. So what else had caught my eye?

I stepped back into the stairwell and shot up to the top floor. With Jennifer covering the exit, I had time to rule it out before returning to the previous level. I returned empty-handed and with no hesitation. No sound or light came from any of the flats. That relegated me to eliminating each one individually. The first door opened at my knock to reveal an overweight man with an allergy to personal hygiene. His level of helpfulness was about equal to his pleasantness. As quickly as possible, I rid myself of him and moved on to the second and third doors with no results. A young woman—a college student, perhaps—

opened the last door. Lucky for me, the coed was a bit of a busybody and recognized my description of Helen right off the bat. A quick conversation later and I stood facing the flat we had spent two weeks looking for: apartment 6C.

As with everything else, the door before me had seen better days. The peeling paint revealed the steel beneath, and the numeral on the door dangled at a precarious angle, held by nothing but a single screw. I tried the handle and got nowhere. I bent over to examine the lock. It was a Durden—cheap, but durable. Silently cursing myself for leaving my lock picks at home in my rush, I reached into my pockets and pulled out my keys. Somewhere on that ring, I had the key to my mother's house. She also used Durden locks. That would work well enough as a start. When I was done, though, I'd need a new key.

As I selected my mother's house key, I paused. Light glinted off the key our mysterious visitor had left outside the office. Durden glistened in engraved letters across the top. I slid it in and twisted. The handle gave easily, and the door opened into a room bathed in a golden glow. Behind me, the stairwell door opened.

The apartment looked like something straight out of the 1970s, with fixtures and appliances to match. To my left sat a galley kitchen, while the rest of the main room was an open living space. Only it was empty. A sallow light filled the room thanks to yellow or yellowed—I couldn't tell which—curtains which framed a picture window on the far wall. A narrow hallway led off to the left. Other than myself, the place was empty.

Well, at least it should have been. At the sound of heavy breathing, I remembered the stairwell door and turned to see Jennifer bent over, chest heaving. She was grinning from ear to ear. "No one down there." The words came out clipped and between breaths. "Tested the elevator. It's at the ground floor. I must have missed them."

I nodded but allowed scorn to temper my voice as I spoke. "Good, but you should never have come up in the first place. Next time, watch the damn exits."

She straightened up, still breathing hard, and placed her hands on her hips in that way all women learn. "And miss all the fun? No way."

I shook my head and moved toward the apartment's back rooms. "Not fun. Work. Don't get them confused again."

The hall was dim but not enough to make much of a difference. Two doorways faced each other. The one on the left was open and the room beyond dark, while the right door remained closed. A sliver of light, much brighter than the warm glow from the main room, speared out from below the door.

From what I could see, the open doorway led to a bathroom. A very scary bathroom. The mirror was cracked, and the tub matched a grimy shower curtain that screamed vintage horror film. The sole towel lay in a ball at the base of the toilet. I shuddered, having no desire to give any of it additional scrutiny.

The closed door wasn't latched, and I used the side of my hand to open it, revealing an extravagantly furnished bedroom. A king-size four-poster bed, its headboard flush with the left wall, took up most of the room. It was flanked by side tables, complete with lamps, and a three-drawer dresser had been shoved into a corner. The bold, red walls matched silk sheets. A black coverlet topped it all off. On the bed lay Helen Black, sprawled in a very unladylike manner. I had to admit the red dress she wore fit her quite well, though the knife jutting from her back seemed to cramp her style.

Behind me, Jennifer gasped. Through gritted teeth, I warned her not to touch anything and held out my hand. "Phone."

She moved slowly and muttered something about it being dead. I flipped the phone over in my hand. God, I hate these things. In order to save a user's information, phones often shut down before the batteries are fully drained. Usually they have enough juice for one quick call. This was one of those cases where I hoped I was right. I pressed the power button.

A moment later, the manufacture's logo popped up, and I let out a breath I didn't know I was holding. As soon as I could, I dialed a number and, after six rings, got the voice I knew best.

"You waited too long." I squatted beside the bed. A hand hung over the side, but I ignored it as I studied the blade sticking out of the body.

Stephanie's voice was tight. "Explain."

"You—as in Stephanie Hawthorne, a private investigator—waited, a verb, too long—as in let too much time pass between thinking about an action and following through with the aforementioned action."

The sound of heaving disrupted Stephanie's return silence. Jennifer, pale and sweating, was bent over, her right hand and the wall the only things keeping her from imminent contact with the floor. Cradling the phone on my shoulder, I grabbed her free arm and hauled her out of the apartment. A dead body—especially one resulting from violent methods—could do that to the most stalwart of people. I returned to the body and the phone call, leaving my niece to handle herself. Time was running short, battery power shorter. Spilling all the details was easier than waiting for Stephanie to ask the questions. It took only a minute and ended with a question of my own. "Instructions?"

"Inform the police. Tell me about the body."

I described it, emphasizing the knife and the dress. "You think that's the same dress from the dry cleaner's?"

"Undoubtedly. Coincidences are too high otherwise. Makeup?"

Helen's face had been done up beautifully. Now, though, it had begun to get a waxy look to it, and with the eyes staring blankly, it unsettled me. I closed my eyes and shook my head to clear it. After a moment, I described it from memory.

"Thank you. Call the police. No. Call James directly. He should be at the office, but if he's not, report it as you see fit. The key will explain your ability to enter. Display it, but relinquish it only if required. Report in as you can." Stephanie hung up.

I shook my head. I've told her numerous times not to end a call like that. She never listens. Pulling James's number from memory, I dialed. He picked up on the third ring. "Hawthorne."

"Daniel," I said, matching his tone. I couldn't help

myself. "Got something I need to talk to you about."

The sound of his grinding teeth could be heard through the phone. "What?"

My chest puffed out as I spoke in a senatorial tone. "The responsibilities placed upon me by citizenship in the United States require me to inform you that I am currently observing the deceased body of one Mrs. Helen Black."

"You sure about that?" The growl got deeper as he went on. "I swear, Atwell, if you're doing this for kicks, I'll stick you in the tank until the sun rises in the west."

"Scout's honor. Pretty sure the knife sticking out of her back is a dead giveaway, though." Pun intended.

"Where you at?"

I gave him the address. "No rush. Don't think she's going anywhere. I'll meet you here."

"Don't touch a thing," James roared before the line went dead. I shrugged and looked at the phone. The screen went black, and it died again. Convenient. I stuck my head out the apartment door and saw Jennifer pacing up and down the hallway. At a lifted eyebrow, she gave me a thumbs-up and I ducked back inside.

Nothing in the apartment indicated it to be anything beyond a discrete hideaway. It lacked all sense of personality and the detritus of life. The kitchen was stocked, if barely. None of the cabinets held anything beyond a moldy loaf of bread, a box of off-brand cereal, and several dozen glasses. The entire stock of dishes—two plates and three bowls—was piled haphazardly in the sink. A drawer next to the wall contained silverware, a mismatched conglomeration that would appear more at home in a thrift store. The knife block on the counter reminded me of another set of knives I'd met earlier. From what I could tell, the remaining knives matched the one temporarily stored in the bedroom. A cabinet above the sink explained why the glasses outnumbered the plates and bowls. Whoever owned this apartment had liked their alcohol, leaving what amounted to a fully stocked bar unprotected.

The inside of the refrigerator reeked, thanks to its only occupant: a gallon of spoiled milk. Or what had once been milk. Its sides bowed outward in an obvious manner, if the clumps in the liquid hadn't given it away.

My perusal of the kitchen complete, I scoped out the living area. Nothing covered the walls, nor were there any signs that furniture had once filled that space. The curtains were shoddy in quality, probably secondhand like the rest of the items in this place. A simple fixture screwed into the wall held them up.

One of the two bathroom lights didn't turn on

when I hit the switch. The walls were painted a shade of olive green last fashionable on army Jeeps in World War II. If possible, the room was even more off-putting in the light. An in-wall medicine cabinet contained only a bottle of aspirin and a mostly empty box of condoms.

I stopped in the bedroom doorway, seeing what lay before me. Seeing, not merely looking. There is a difference between the two, and don't let any wordsmith or teacher convince you otherwise. In common vernacular, they may be interchangeable in most situations. But in practice, they are two entirely separate concepts.

The red walls infused the room with a sense of passion. The lampshades were also red, probably meant to enhance the mood. I had no doubt that the bed, and the activities it supported, was the focus of the room. It sat in a prominent location, and obvious care had been used in its placement. Odds on the room's significance doubled, considering the state of the rest of the apartment and that this room looked habitable, if not well-kept.

The side tables were simple but elegant affairs. Wooden statues with carved legs, they consisted of nothing more than a flat space on top of four posts. Each supported a lamp but was bare otherwise, save for a single digital clock that blinked twelve at me. A narrow closet opposite the bed deserved further scrutiny.

The bed drew the bulk of my attention. The sheets were silk, luxuriant, and—I assumed—expensive. Their dark red hue matched the rest of the room, yet provided a slight contrast. Don't ask me to explain how that works. Matching red pillows accentuated the black coverlet which topped the bed. Four intricately carved wooden posts jutted up from the bed frame. One was cracked near the headboard, and, upon closer inspection, slight wear marks were visible on all four posts where they'd rubbed against the thick, pillow-top mattress. Interesting.

Helen's body lay diagonally across the bed. Her right arm dangled over the side at the elbow, while her left angled up by her head. Despite the intrusion of the knife blade, this was my first chance to see the infamous red dress. A hip-high slit up the right side revealed a bare leg bent at a lewd angle. The bottom half was bunched beneath her, exposing most of her left thigh. Red, strapped, stiletto heels finished off the ensemble.

I turned away from the bed and focused on the closet. Using a handkerchief-covered hand, I pulled on the handle to expose an array of dresses in different colors and cuts. Each seemed to be the same size, but with different purposes in mind. A business suit hung adjacent to a formal dress. Sequins next to stripes next to solids. Shoes, mostly heeled affairs, sat in pairs on the floor and were just as varied as the dresses.

Lingerie of all shapes, colors, and materials filled the dresser's top drawer. Stuffed was a better word. I shuffled through it all before closing the drawer with my hip. More lingerie filled the second drawer, along with an interesting collection of adult toys. The bottom drawer had significantly more heft to it, and I heard police sirens out front by the time I had it open.

I expected to find more of the same, but books filled the space instead, each without a dust jacket. I pawed through them before shoving the drawer closed and running out of the apartment. What was interesting was that all the books were personal. And I'm talking about personal on an emotional and individual level. The collection of well-worn children's books and other texts, when combined into a unified whole, looked much like a childhood stuffed into one drawer. Handing such information off to the police without fully exploring it displeased me.

I stepped out of the apartment and glanced about the hallway. Jennifer had disappeared, but I had no time to look for her. The numbers above the elevator ticked upward. Shutting the door firmly behind me, I chose a place next to the doorway and used my back to support it.

Flipping a half dollar I'd found in my pocket completed the look—or at least as much as it could without a suit and fedora. The elevator dinged, and James shot out before the doors finished opening.

He hates it when I stand like this. One year, in a fit of uncharacteristic brotherliness over two bottles of tequila, he explained it to me. In his mind, that pose is the quintessential private dick and screams something suspicious. It drives him nuts. That's why I do it.

Every. Chance. I. Get.

James strode up to me, nostrils flaring, and snatched the coin out of the air before jabbing his forefinger at me. "What the hell is going on?" His posse fanned out behind him, sniffing around the place like a pack of bloodhound pups with no clue what they were looking for. "She in there?"

"If I tell you, may I pretty please have my coin back?" I crossed my arms. "It's lucky."

"If it's so lucky, you can thank it for me not hauling you in for obstructing a police investigation." James turned to the nearest officer, one of the few to actually find the right door, and ordered him to open it.

The officer looked dumbfounded for a second. There were obvious implications if this wasn't handled correctly. I stepped in front of both of them and spoke up.

"Let me."

James shot me a look as he barreled past me, almost all of his cronies following. I stayed put, resuming my place beside the jamb. Across the hallway, the coed's door opened and Jennifer slipped out. She made a move to join me, but I shook my head. She nodded before heading for the stairwell. Hopefully, she remembered her standing instructions to report back to Stephanie.

Half a minute later, James strode out of the apartment. "She's dead."

"Noticed that, did you? Glad to know my detective skills are still up to snuff. It was close there, with that knife and all."

James scowled. "How'd you learn about the body?"

"It was there when I walked in."

Grunt. "You randomly break into strangers' apartments? And one that conveniently contains the body of a woman we both know? A woman who, by the way, is connected to a case we are both working on? Why don't I believe you?"

"Because your job has made you jaded against innate goodness and random chance. Can I have my coin back?"

"No," James snarled, "but you can have an all-expenses-paid trip down to the station and answer some questions." He barked out a name, and the officer I'd assisted in opening the door appeared at his side. "Escort Mr. Atwell down to headquarters. He has some information he'd like to share."

The officer reached out and grabbed my arm at the elbow. I responded by pulling loose and stepping back. "Hey now, is that any way to treat a friend, an informant, and a potential gym buddy? I'm gaining a little extra around the middle and could do with some time there, if you want to join me. I hate going alone. Besides, your boss still has my coin. Half dollars aren't easy to find."

"So go to the bank for another."

I shook my head. "Not happening. And that goes double for the trip downtown, while we're at it. If you got questions, I'll answer them the best I can—but at my leisure, not yours, and definitely not downtown. Arrest me if you want, but I won't go willingly, copper." The last bit came out in a bad James Cagney

The officer looked at James who growled deep in his throat. "Wait here. Keep an eye on him. He moves, arrest him as a material witness. I'll be right back." James ducked back into the apartment.

His definition of "right back" and mine were polar opposites. I stayed put, leaning against the wall again, my would-be jailer's eyes never leaving me. That was fine, just as long as it was his eyes and not his hands. Time crept by. He never moved, but I did, eventually taking a seat on the floor. I entertained myself the best I could. When making personal constellations out of the dots on the ceiling tiles got boring, I switched to playing silly games in my head. Sure, I could have thought about the case, but I didn't want to assist James in any way. Besides, thinking was Stephanie's end of the business. How could I, her loving husband, take that from her?

After an hour and a half, I'd had enough. I started singing. I couldn't carry a tune in a bucket, but I knew the words and belted out something written by Tom Waits at the top of my lungs. This created the desired effect. During my isolation, a football team of police and men in white coats had arrived, until roughly twenty people milled about the place, all dusting, sweeping, and looking for clues. My singing stopped it all in one fell swoop.

Seconds later, James shot out of the apartment. "Get him outta here!" His finger shot out at me. Two cronies rushed to comply, and I let them haul me to my feet. Once there, though, I shook off their hands, straightened my clothing, and then walked to the elevator, singing all the while. They escorted me; one even hit the ground floor button. I paused long enough to say thank you before resuming. No reason to be rude.

I left the same way I came in—through the front door and under my own power. Standing on the stoop, I took a moment to adjust to my current circumstances. The street outside was certainly much busier than when I first arrived. A dozen police cruisers were now parked haphazardly along the street. Jennifer was nowhere to be seen. Shrugging, I started toward my car and home.

Chapter 16

"There is no shame in feeling squeamish around a dead body."

The sun was setting as I pulled into the garage. I was exhausted, and I knew Stephanie would have questions. Weariness washed over me at the thought of it. Still, I knew I had to fill her in on the afternoon's events.

I ignored the office as I walked down the hall to the front room. Stephanie was probably in there, reading a book or working on some knitting project, but I wanted to close everything down first. I figured Stephanie might have forgotten; she had, so I shut the blinds and locked the door. Returning to the office took more time than it should have, but entering explained the building's pervading silence.

Jennifer sat in one of the chairs before Stephanie's desk, head down and elbows on knees. Stephanie sat silent behind her desk. They both looked up at my entrance, and Jennifer ran to me, enveloping me in a bear hug which I gladly returned. Reaching into my pocket, I returned her phone before collapsing into my chair.

Stephanie's eyes held something akin to concern

as she looked at me. "Jennifer wanted to go back for you. I convinced her it was not wise."

I pulled a bottle and a glass I saved for special occasions from the bottom drawer of my desk. After I poured two fingers and took a healthy sip, I suppressed a shudder before I spoke—not to Stephanie, but Jennifer. "You stay away from James and the police. At least for now. You're not ready for them."

I could tell Jennifer wanted to say something, but she could read the room well enough to stay quiet. As for Stephanie . . . I was feeling a bit defensive. "Try searching an apartment in ten minutes flat for something you aren't sure exists—without leaving a trace, mind you—then wait for three hours as the police search the same apartment, intent upon finding enough evidence to offer you a room downtown for the night. It wears you out."

Stephanie snorted as she lifted her glass for a sip. I hadn't noticed it before. See? Tired. "What happened?"

I sat back and nursed my drink, relating everything that occurred after I left the office. Jennifer blushed when I suggested she got ill at the sight of Helen, but I flashed her a wink and a smile and just kept going. When I reached the end of my tale, I also reached the bottom of my glass. The bottle sang a siren's song, but I put it away and fetched some water from the refrigerator instead.

Stephanie said nothing for a bit, just sat with eyes closed. Jennifer looked confused. She opened her mouth to speak, but I patted her shoulder and shook my head as I returned to my seat, quieting her for the moment. When Stephanie opened her eyes, she focused them on Jennifer.

"There is no shame in feeling squeamish around a dead body, especially one in such a state. It's a risk our trade takes. Be aware of that. You may never see one again, or you may never overcome the physical illness it brings, but if it does happen, do your best to control yourself and the situation. Your uncle acted correctly in removing you from the room. Had I been there, I would've done the same—in both your cases."

Jennifer looked confused for a moment before understanding dawned. I had intended to speak with her about that myself, but perhaps I need not now. Stephanie had covered it, and the girl did listen to her aunt. Jennifer just sat in the chair, legs drawn up, and accepted the judgment without a word. She was good at heart. She'd be fine.

I changed the subject. "Did you learn anything useful from that coed?"

My niece shook her head. "Unc, don't call her a coed. Sounds like something straight out of a porno flick." I shrugged and Jennifer went on. "Nothing of any importance, really. She says she doesn't know what happened in the apartment. Helen wasn't the only woman she saw come and go regularly. She described another. Sounded a lot like Andrea Swope to me. Both would come and go at odd hours, always with different men."

"Did she seem credible?" Stephanie said.

"She appeared to be working on some sort of schooling—a doctorate in chemistry, I think she said. She works weird hours at her school as a lab assistant. But beyond that, nothing about her or her apartment indicated she was lying. There wasn't much in the place other than chemistry books. I looked. No television, no movies, nothing but more books. There's no way I could live like that."

Stephanie snorted. "You live like you have to. Don't assume your uncle and I have always lived this way. Nor is this how we intend to spend the rest of our lives. You do what you can—however you can—with what you have, until you can better yourself."

Jennifer would learn that truth in her own time. I changed the subject again. "Did you head back here directly after I told you to leave?"

I expected Jennifer to answer, but this time Stephanie cut in. "Yes. She did. It was well done." Jennifer preened at the compliment. "Now, however, it's time for her to go. I already called Logan off, and her mother will be wondering where she is soon."

Jennifer got the hint, though I could tell leaving wasn't her first choice. I saw her out and relocked the door behind her. Standing in the office doorway, I caught Stephanie's eye, and with an ostentatious glance at my watch, flicked off the lights and left her sitting at her desk.

By the time Stephanie arrived upstairs, I lay sprawled on the couch, remote in hand, listening more than watching the evening news. She set my half-finished glass of water on the coffee table and headed for the kitchen. She returned with her own glass and curled up next to me on the couch.

"What's going on?" If I wasn't mistaken, her quiet concern was sincere.

My mood, with plenty of time to fester, now ruled my emotional landscape. "I almost had it. I'm sure of it. The answer we've been looking for was somewhere in that room, but I couldn't find it before your brother arrived. Might as well fire me now." Crossing my arms, I turned back to the news.

Self-destructive streaks are like that—self-destructive.

"He didn't even ask how I got into the apartment." I pulled the key from my pocket and showed it to Stephanie. "Would've thought that might be an important piece of information."

Stephanie beamed as she took the key. That meant something . . . and usually something good. "You're right," she said. "That room held what we were looking for. James will have what I need to figure it all out. Contact him tomorrow and see what he wants in return."

"What if he won't cough it up?"

She finished her water and set the glass down beside mine. "He will. James is no idiot, but he can—and often does—ignore salient facts which refuse to match his view of events, even when those facts are so obvious I'm surprised he fails to trip over them."

Helen Swope's murder kicked off the next hour's broadcast.

Chapter 17

"I don't know how much you helped, but my day sure as hell isn't any brighter from seeing you."

My phone call to Stephanie's brother never happened. It was a slow morning, with Stephanie sleeping in until breakfast while I putzed around. It was well past ten when the two of us took our seats in the office. Then the door opened and I was back up again. I escorted James into the office.

I didn't have to direct him to a seat; he took one for himself, turning it so he could see both of us with as little effort as possible. Stephanie frowned. She didn't like anyone rearranging her office without permission. This behavior was unusual. Normally, James focused on Stephanie and ignored me, but yesterday's escapades must have irked him.

He scooted forward to the edge of the chair for his opening remarks. "I want to know how you knew Helen Black was in that apartment." He pointed at me, jabbing the air with every word.

"James!" Stephanie's voice shot out like the crack

of a whip. "Our mother taught you better than that. Try again."

"Oh will you please shut up for once? A woman's dead, and what do I find but your husband standing over the body. I think I have the right to know. That's my job. Now kindly keep your trap shut, or I'll haul you both downtown."

I put my feet up on a corner of my desk. "Two things. One: I was not standing over the body. I met you at the door and let you in since your lackey couldn't figure out how a doorknob works. Two: Your question was a statement and, as such, requires no rebuttal unless I wish to make one."

"Why, I ought to . . ." James was on his feet in an instant, jaw clenched. "Listen up, wiseass. Quit your dissembling and answer the implied questions, too. I'm doing you a favor. Next time I'll just book you as a material witness and see how much you like my accommodations."

Before I could speak, Stephanie jumped in. "Sit down, James. Daniel, explain it to him."

I proceeded to do so, unloading everything from the discovery of the apartment building to the key I found outside. But I refused to elaborate on the subject more than I had to. If he believed something different than what

I said, it was on him.

"Do you still have it? I want to see that key." James's words were still snappy, but they held a little less bite. I fetched it from my key ring and tossed it to him. "You've ruined any prints on here. You know that, right? I have to take this as evidence pertaining to an ongoing police investigation."

"Fine with me. I made a copy last week." There was no copy. You know this, but James didn't. It's enjoyable watching him flush with anger.

"You willing to answer some questions for me now?"

I glanced at Stephanie and she nodded. "Possibly. Do I get my coin back?"

"Damn your coin. You've explained why you were at the apartment. I want more. You remove anything?"

"I know better than that. Saw the body. Called you."

"A neighbor said you weren't alone. A young woman in her late teens was with you? Sounded suspiciously like your niece."

"You know what she looks like as well as I. Why ask?"

"I want to hear it from you. She doesn't have a license. If she isn't careful . . ." He left the rest unsaid.

"What was her part in all this?"

I glanced at Stephanie. She was leaning back in her chair with her eyes closed. But she must have expected my question, because she nodded once before I could even ask it. James snapped as I turned back to him. "Don't look at her. I'm in charge here. Now answer the damn question." Stephanie opened one eye, lizard-like, and scowled at her brother before closing it again.

The questioning went on. Stephanie said next to nothing the entire time, as James focused his energy on me. Twice she stepped in to request clarification when we touched on the red dress. Apparently, that bit of fabric held more significance than I realized.

James stood and stretched. "I don't know how much you helped, but my day sure as hell isn't any brighter from seeing you."

"One moment, please." Stephanie opened her eyes and focused on James. "I have one favor I'd like to request."

Looking down at her, James smirked. "You're not in much of a position to ask for favors, but this might be amusing. What do you want?"

"I assume I won't be allowed in that apartment. I'd like to see a list of everything you found there, no matter how trivial. You usually have lists for everything.

Passing one along should not be too much trouble."

I could see the calculations swirling behind James's eyes. If he could make heads or tails of it, he was doing better than I. Something about that room had piqued Stephanie's curiosity, and I'd be damned if I knew what it was.

Eventually he agreed. "All right. Swing by in a day or two, and I'll see what I can do."

Stephanie shook her head. "Not good enough."

"It damn well better be. Feel lucky that you're getting anything."

"We will be by later today." Stephanie acted as if James hadn't spoken. "Good day."

James grunted, and I followed as he stomped from the office. When I returned, Stephanie stood at the window with her hands clasped behind her back. I walked up, wrapping my arms around her from behind. My intrusion didn't cause a stir, though she tilted her head back to rest on my shoulder.

We stood there for a while, neither of us saying a word. It was pleasant. And over too soon. "I need to speak with Mr. Swope," she said, walking around me and out of the office.

I followed her to the garage. "You know, there's this newfangled invention called a phone. You could just call him. And which Swope are we talking about?"

"Both, if possible." She climbed into the passenger side of my car. A bit presumptuous, that. I slid behind the wheel as expected. Despite my continued questioning, Stephanie kept silent regarding her intentions with the Swopes. Of course, this didn't stop my own theories from flying through my head, though those seldom held any weight when Stephanie became involved. Eventually, I just gave up and focused on the road.

The waiting room looked much the same as my last visit, the only difference being the bodies that filled most of the open space. Some were clients, or soon would be, but the vast majority were reporters. Public announcement of another murder within the Swope family must have rekindled interest in Andrea's death.

Miss Swanson stood at the front of the crowd, hands upraised in a futile attempt to corral the unruly mob. Her already flushed face darkened when we entered, her eyes glued only on us. Two reporters tried to capitalize on her distraction by sneaking around her desk. Hands flashed out as she shoved them back into their colleagues, causing a group to hit the floor.

Stephanie ignored all this, circling the reporters and sidestepping Swanson. I'm sure Swope's secretary wanted to stop us, but another group of reporters swarmed forward. I shrugged apologetically as she glared at us over her shoulder.

We hit the elevator without stopping. Once inside, Stephanie punched the button for the top floor. As the doors shut, I saw Swanson reach for her desk phone. The elevator rose, and I gave it a count of three before hitting the stop button.

"Which Swope do you want to see first?" I returned Stephanie's glare easily enough. "They're on different floors. Besides, I bet one of them isn't even here."

"Such are the risks we run." What kind of answer was that? "Take me to our client. His silence regarding our investigation is surprising."

I nodded and hit the button for the top floor. Soon enough, we stood in the hallway outside Arthur Swope's massive office. I swung his door open without bothering to knock. The firm's namesake sat behind his desk, glasses perched on the tip of his nose. Returning his scowl with smile number four, I closed the door and escorted Stephanie to a pair of grand armchairs before his desk.

"Heather told me you'd arrived." Arthur Swope sat back and crossed his arms. "You should have talked to her. I am not in the mood for chicanery or interruption.

And somehow, I doubt your appearance is unrelated to my daughter-in-law's death."

Stephanie nodded. "I'm sorry for your loss."

"What loss was it to me? She wasn't my wife. My wife has been dead for over six months, and you are supposed to be finding her killer, not bothering me."

A smile flashed across Stephanie's face, though it failed to reach her eyes. "About that. I am surprised at your lack of interest. Most clients refuse to allow us a moment's peace, yet you are the opposite. Quite an oddity."

"Why would you want my interference? You do your job, and I have no reason to call you, visit you, or otherwise contact you. Would you prefer it otherwise? If not, then shut up and let me get on with my work while you do the same."

This provoked a moment of silence from Stephanie. When she spoke again, her voice was chilled. "I would expect you to be with your son today, Mr. Swope."

The firm's namesake snorted. "With who? Robert?" He shook his head. "He's a man. He doesn't need me around. Why should I waste time on his problems?"

Stephanie's response was calm, cool, and collected, holding no obvious condemnation. Exactly the opposite of my current state of mind. I was livid. A father should be with his son in his time of grief, not studying legal briefs. Unfortunately, that same anger also prevented me from hearing Stephanie's response.

Swope took off his glasses in a grand gesture of frustration. "Listen. I am *here* because things demand my attention. I am *here* because I have a business to run. I am *here* because Robert is grieving, and his cases need to be distributed to more competent lawyers. I am *not* with him because he is a big boy and can handle himself. The man is already at my house and will probably stay there until I kick him out. Again. So, if you have some other criticism, spit it out. Otherwise, get out of here and do the job I hired you to do."

Just like that, Stephanie was on her feet and out the door, the suddenness of it catching me flat-footed. It took me a moment to react. The elevator door was open, and she was halfway inside by the time I caught up with her. "Odds on mariticide just went up," I said on the way down. "It's five to one. Place your bets now."

Stephanie grunted. "I have no doubt that he either knows or suspects something. It matters little now. There are other concerns which hold my attention."

I shrugged. "Agree to disagree. That whole conversation fairly reeked of condemnation—for us, for

Robert, for the whole situation. It's almost as if he doesn't care if either murder is ever solved."

The elevator dinged and the doors opened. Nothing had changed in the lobby, and Stephanie and I dodged around the crowd. Swanson said nothing to us as we passed by, probably because it would have been picked up, written down, and published by the fourteen million reporters in the room. If looks could kill, though….

Stephanie pushed open the outside doors. "The question is why he no longer cares. After the passion he showed upon hiring us, his apathy is interesting. Why express such distain now?"

We continued to talk as we returned to the car. In actuality, it was more me pestering Stephanie for answers she didn't have. Curiosity doesn't often get the better of me, but at that moment I didn't particularly care. Stephanie kept her peace, refusing to answer any of my questions, even if she did have the answers.

She got into the car with a sigh and a single question of her own. Unfortunately, I had no idea when James would have that list for Helen Black's secret apartment.

My answer wasn't what she wanted to hear. Stephanie worked on her own time and cursed whoever interfered with it. I could not only hear her foot tapping, but I could feel the car shift with the vibrations. Putting my hand on her right knee, I stopped both.

Stephanie turned to look at me with angry eyes over pouted lips. "You wanted to talk to both father and son," I reminded her. "Why don't we go see Robert?" It wasn't a great idea. Really no more than a stopgap, but it was good enough. She nodded and I started the car.

Chapter 18

"She was a whore."

Robert's car, the same one he'd driven to the office five weeks ago, sat in his father's driveway. Nothing about it or the house appeared different. As soon as the car stopped, Stephanie jumped out and headed toward the door. I took my time, following at a more discrete distance. Everything about Stephanie's body language screamed that, to paraphrase popular culture, the game was afoot. That, I must admit, piqued my interest.

Reaching the front stoop, Stephanie raised her hand to knock, but the door flew open before she could do so. What was left of Robert Swope stood before us. Gone was the mousy man I'd met inside the law offices. Instead, he was a comparative ghost, with sunken cheeks and suspicious eyes that flicked about as if searching for some danger just out of view. His once well-kept hair, still thick with mousse, now had a mind of its own, jutting about with no grand consensus among the lot. Stubble blurred his jawline, more grey on display than one might expect.

But the worst part was his eyes. They'd never struck me as particularly merry, but now what little light had been there was extinguished. Red rimmed, they drew the eye, even as the rest of him pushed you away. It wasn't depression that pulled you in; it was the haunted cast which seemed soul-deep.

He glared at us as he held the door open, and I nodded my thanks as we crossed the threshold. Stephanie said nothing—nor did she wipe her feet—as she made a beeline down the hall and entered one room after another, Robert and I strolling along behind her. I pulled Robert aside as Stephanie entered the kitchen.

"Have you slept?" I asked, searching his eyes for a reaction. Slowly at first, but then with more enthusiasm, his head bobbed, as if it needed to build momentum first.

"No."

"I know you aren't going to listen to me, but I'm going to tell you all the same. Get some rest. It helps." I let go of his arm and ushered him into the kitchen.

We found Stephanie inside, reintroducing herself to the seemingly ever-present cat. It sunned itself on a window sill, while Stephanie ran her hand down its back.

Robert stopped dead seeing the two. "Catherine doesn't let strangers near her, let alone pet her. She must like you."

I crossed my arms as I leaned against the counter. "She has good taste. Catherine seems like an odd name for a cat."

Robert shrugged. "Mom's idea of a joke. She knew we'd end up calling her Cat, so this way it made more sense. Cat can't stand Father. I'm surprised he's kept her this long, but I'm glad he did. She gives me something to remember Mom by." He reached out to scratch the cat's head, which was a tad more attention than the feline preferred. We watched her saunter from the room, though Robert seemed oblivious to her exit. He walked over to the sink and filled a glass of water for himself, downing it in one long swallow before repeating and taking a seat at the dining room table.

Robert folded his hands in his lap and stared at the floor, neck bent and head drooping. "I suppose you're here about Helen."

Stephanie took a seat across from Robert, though he didn't seem to notice. "Yes. Let me express our sympathies."

"Thank you. At least someone . . ."

"I expect others regret Helen's passing."

"Probably." Robert shook his head as he spoke. "Who's to say? She . . . she was a runaway. I never met her parents, but I suppose they'd be sad if they knew. I wish

I'd known them. Just to tell them that their daughter had a good life. Kind of odd, the things we wish for when we're grieving and can't have what we really want."

"I understand. But I still need some information from you. Be aware that a few of my questions will sting or offend. I assure you, however, a method exists, and I ask that you bear with me. Are you willing?" She waited for Robert's nod. "Good. Now tell me why you are at your father's house."

Robert shifted uncomfortably. "I didn't want to be alone."

"Yet here you are. Alone."

"You know how close my father and I are. Despite my best efforts, we've always been that way. I think it stems from his childhood . . . but it doesn't matter, I guess. When I need him, he comes through in his own way. Like letting me stay here for a few days."

"Why?"

"I don't know. Maybe I've been a failure in his eyes. No matter what I do, no matter how well I perform, nothing is good enough for that man. There were times I cried myself to sleep wanting his approval. At first I thought he just wanted to push me, but as I got older it never changed."

"Nonsense," Stephanie said. "If he disapproves of

you so much, why are you here?"

"I convinced him to let me stay. My entire place reminds me of Helen, and that's too painful right now. I want to be someplace where I can't see her with every turn of my head. Somewhere I can remember happier times. He understands that." Robert looked up at Stephanie and shrugged. "Like this place. Everything about it reminds me of simpler times.

"*Allowing* me to join the firm was strictly politics. It was expected of him, and Father always does what is expected of him. It was *expected* that he pay for college, so he did. When I chose his field and became a lawyer, it was *expected* that he would hire me. So he did."

"Tell me about your wife."

"What is there to tell? You met her yourself."

"I barely spoke to her, let alone formed any conclusions." I knew that for a lie, but didn't interrupt. "Besides, your experiences with her were much more extensive than mine; you knew her longer and much more intimately."

"Despite what most people thought, she was a loving woman. She was just jaded. Life did that to her."

"What about your friends? Your coworkers? How did they interact?"

The interrogation came to a halt as Robert

collapsed in tears, throwing his hands up to cover his face. Neither of us moved. Why the intense reaction to such routine questions?

Stephanie let the crying continue for a few minutes before pressing on. "Mr. Swope?"

"They hated her!" Spittle spewed from Robert's mouth as his head whipped up, his words tainted by their feral ferocity. "They hated her. They thought she had me fooled, but I knew who she was—*what* she was—and I loved her all the same. It was just a job. That's all it was. Mere physicality. And I was all right with it." He broke down in tears again.

In other circumstances, it might seem rude to press on such an open wound, but it needed to be done. Both Stephanie and I realized this. We weren't the police, forced to play nice to grieving widowers. Stephanie's voice was hard as she spoke. Clearly, vagueness did not please her. "What are you talking about?"

Robert mumbled something. Neither of us caught it, and Stephanie asked him to repeat himself. "She was a whore. A prostitute." Another sob escaped his lips in the ensuing silence.

What do you say to that?

After a minute, Robert went on. "Or a madam who still occasionally performed her own tricks. I was never sure. She kept me away from it all. She said business was business, and we were personal, and never should the two mix. And I believed her. I let her do what she wanted as long as she came home at the end of the day. Still came back to me. And she did, day after day, always wonderful.

"But everyone held it against her. Friends. Family. It didn't matter. Father never seemed to care much, but Mom did. She was always fickle about it—disapproving one day, accepting another.

"So, yes, I knew about the apartment. Where it was, I had no idea. She always said privacy was king in that business. The flat's isolation was paramount. I never asked to see it. Do you think one of her clients did this to her? If I'd known, then maybe—"

"You'd have done what, Mr. Swope? There was nothing you could do. Nothing you knew or did not know would have changed the outcome. Do not go beating yourself up for something over which you had no control. Did you inform the police about your wife's profession?"

Robert's whole body shook as he answered. "No. You don't just go around telling people your wife's a madam. Besides, that lot discriminates. Another dead hooker is the last thing on their to-do list. I can't divulge that information to some knuckle-dragger. How would it affect this family? Helen wouldn't want that. She'd understand my concern for the family's reputation. More importantly, she'd be concerned about the reputations of her clientele."

Stephanie stood, all trace of sympathy gone. "Your silence only assists her murderer. Such information will always come out, given time. If you truly want to honor her memory, then I suggest you contact the authorities and inform them of what you just told me. They have a strong distaste for liars, as do I. Save yourself the complications and go to them before they come to you. That is my advice, Mr. Swope." She left the room, disgust evident in her footfalls.

That seemed a bit harsh to me, but I followed Stephanie out of the house. Once in the car, I made a comment to that effect. She ignored me, so I dropped it after the one go. There were better times for such things.

Of course, those times might be more obvious if I had dared look at my wife. She sat there, lost in thought, white-knuckled hands clasped tight. I finally spoke up, tired of waiting, and questioned her intentions for the rest of the day's activities. Stephanie blinked herself back to the present and spoke with a storm's fury in her eyes.

"These people! How do they make the assumption that their lives are better than yours or mine? Refusing to tell the police about your wife's activities based solely on appearances? Why? Isn't justice more important? Revenge? Punishing those who have done wrong to you and yours? These are the emotions that rule humanity, yet they deny them, claiming their clay is of a rarer quality. So much nonsense. They are no better than you or me or my brother or your niece."

"You despise them, yet you still work for them. A bit hypocritical, don't you think?"

Stephanie glared at me. I could see the question behind her eyes. Whose side was I on?

We sat in silence as I maneuvered the car down city streets. When I get that look, sane policy is to back off and let her have some space—mentally, if not physically. But after a while, it starts to chafe. Everything from the set of her jaw to the look in her eye gets under my skin and starts to itch something fierce. Once the itching starts, the clock begins ticking, and sooner or later, I'll say something. I lasted all of three minutes this time.

"What's on your mind?"

Surprisingly enough, the answer came back relatively fast and, more impressively, civil to boot.

"What kind of husband ignores all information regarding his wife's profession in order to respect her privacy? And what kind of man can disregard jealousy and other primal emotions regarding that form of profession?"

"So you've turned into a marriage counselor now?"

She shook her head. "I am merely attempting to answer some questions. The answers may be simple, but to assume so without consideration would be folly."

"Shouldn't you be more concerned with figuring out who killed Andrea?"

Stephanie looked at me with a face full of innocent confusion. "Why? The two murders are connected."

"Wait. What?"

"Which cliché do you want me to use? To assume otherwise seems folly. It's conjecture at this point, but only because I lack proof. Mrs. Black's death is connected to Mrs. Swope's. She knew her murderer—and that of her mother-in-law. That information got her killed."

I drove on in silence for a bit. I could see the possibility of a connection, but if she was really a hooker . . . It was too much for me. "Spill it."

She refused. "Not at this juncture. Besides, other equally important questions require answers as well. Once we have them, we will see which pieces fit where."

Ten minutes later, I pulled to a stop and parked the car down the street from the police station. If my gut was right, and what we needed was in Helen's apartment,

Stephanie could find it here. I understood the eagerness to get her hands on that list. Hell, I was just as anxious.

Chapter 19

"Tripe, Mr. Hunt. I can and I will."

We found James sifting through a mountain of paperwork at his desk and received no more than a grunt at our entrance. Stephanie took the same seat I'd occupied on my previous visit; I chose to stand, facing out the office window. We waited, neither sibling intent upon being the first to give in and begin the conversation. Three minutes and fifteen seconds later—yes, I was timing them—James broke the silence.

"Stephanie," said James.

"James." I'll give you three guesses who that was.

"What do you want?"

Snort. "You know what I want." *I* wanted to lecture Stephanie about flies, honey, and vinegar.

"I don't have it."

"Why?"

"Because I don't." James scowled. "Choose your reason; I got plenty of them. Let's just say I have several active cases, each with family, the public, or some elected official breathing down my neck. Your request's not top priority. Nor is the death of a hooker."

"You knew she was a prostitute?" Stephanie's voice was flat.

"Your lack of surprise is noted. Yes, I did. We're keeping this one close. Her death might not be related to the Swope murder, but I suspect it is."

Stephanie snorted. "There is little question of that. At least you are still able to see the obvious. You should, unless you cheated on Mother's tests."

I heard a slap—not the skin-on-skin kind, but rather skin against wood. "You ask for a favor and then insult me. You damn well know better than that. All you private dicks are the same—asking the police to do your work for you and then claiming all the credit. Well, not this time. Out! Both you and that child you married."

I turned toward the door—not because of James's orders, but because of a knock. A few steps across the room and I pulled it open. On the other side stood a female officer, dressed in a uniform that I fully appreciated in both color and cut. She took a step back and brought a manila folder protectively to her chest.

"Thank you." James reached over my shoulder and tugged it from her grasp. Closing the door, I watched as he perused the file while returning to his desk. Plucking a single sheet from the mess, he dropped it on Stephanie's lap. She took it without a word. Her finger traced down the page, words forming silently on her lips. A moment later, Stephanie's finger tapped the page before she handed it back to James.

"Find what you were looking for?" James asked as he thrust everything into a desk drawer.

Stephanie changed the subject. "How did you know Helen was a prostitute?"

"You see one love nest, you've seen 'em all. Sure, they come in different varieties, but they're all similar in their own ways. My gut told me what it was as soon as Daniel opened the door. But you were about as unsurprised as you can get at her activities. How'd you know?"

That sounded almost polite coming from James. Stephanie ignored it. "Suffice it to say that my source is more reliable than your instincts. I know what faith you have in your gut. You'll have it, soon enough. Do you plan on releasing Helen's career choice to the public?"

"Why do you care?"

"I represent Mr. Swope and his interests. That information would damage him and his reputation as an upstanding citizen and directly hinder his ability to earn a living."

"And his ability to pay you. That's not my

problem, but officially, we do not have any intention of it for the time being, until and unless it becomes necessary."

"Agreed."

"That was no bargain," James countered. "Just a statement of fact. The decision to release the information is mine and mine alone. You have no say." The last words were measured and paced with deliberate malice.

"That, I believe, will hardly matter by the end of this." Stephanie stood. "In fact, I doubt it will matter by the end of the week."

"Why the end of the week? What are you holding back?" James asked. "Do you know who killed Helen Black?"

"No." The word was abrupt, a gunshot. "I have no proof. To act without it would be slander. But I can tell you this: it's the same person who killed Mrs. Swope. The second murder was a mistake—one to capitalize on. Phui. A week is much longer than will be required. Don't be surprised if I have him trussed for you by the end of the day. I need to go."

"Like hell you will." James rounded his desk to confront us. I say us, though he only had eyes for Stephanie. "Tell me the murderer's name, and I'll find out if you're right or not. You don't and I'll book you as a material witness. Strip you of your license."

"Wouldn't do you any good with me," I said from my spot next to the door. "No matter how many slivers you put under my fingernails or bones you break, I won't spill it. Mostly that's because I can't tell you what I don't know, but there's the principle behind it. What I can tell you, however, is what I had for breakfast: two eggs, scrambled with cheese."

Stephanie snorted as she jerked a thumb at me. "He has no idea who your murderer is. Arresting him would be pointless. Daniel might even enjoy the change of pace. But no, I have nothing to give you right now."

James kept quiet as I escorted Stephanie from the room. Even after we left, I felt his eyes on my back, quickening my step. Part of me expected him to call for our detention until he got what he wanted.

I felt no relief until we reached the car and I dropped into the driver's seat. "Where to now?"

Stephanie reclined the passenger seat as far as it would go and closed her eyes. "The library should have what I need."

I started the car. "You know, you could have driven today. Why am I stuck behind the wheel while you get to nap?"

Stephanie cracked an eye and glared out at me. "I thought all men preferred driving. Doesn't chauffeuring a woman around stroke your ego?" I shut up and focused on the drive.

The two-story public library stood only ten minutes from our office. Its exterior was more imposing than the inside would suggest. Standing before it, one got an impression of its steadfast ability to weather the ravages of time; inside, the librarians weren't so lucky. They were a kindly group, made up mostly of older women whose antics were lost on the likes of me. It was a second home to Stephanie. I supported the library, if in spirit more than in fact, but rarely entered the halls.

When we arrived, Stephanie motioned for me to stay put. This left me with my thoughts and a choice: radio or silence. Silence won out, and I dropped my seat back, giving my mind full reign.

Things were moving fast now, faster than I expected. What had Stephanie seen on that list? She hadn't volunteered the information, but I felt sure it was exactly what I'd missed during my search. Sure, I could have asked, but other questions flitted through my mind. Why would Helen store personal belongings in a love nest rather than at home, safe from the prying eyes of her guests? The simple answer was that she didn't trust Robert. Why? He was her husband. Wives should be able to trust their husbands, not keep secrets from them. And if that was the case, what was the secret?

I suspected Stephanie knew the answer to that one. Everything from her body language to her speech patterns said she knew something. She would soon tell me what was going on; she had to if she wanted to pull off "The Big Reveal." If I knew anything about my wife, she loved a good show, especially if she was at the center of it all.

Twenty or so minutes later, Stephanie emerged carrying a single sheet of paper. It flipped in the wind as she yanked open her door and slid into the passenger seat. One glance at her and I righted my seat and started the car.

Stephanie said nothing during the drive back to the office. I didn't press her for details, but I wanted to. There were no overt signs, no yelling or screaming, no anger etching her face. She knew something. I knew the look: face carefully controlled but with eyes of a tempest.

No words were exchanged until we sat behind our desks. I had helped myself to a drink upon our return, but Stephanie chose the stale pop she'd left on her desk from the night before. Spinning in my chair to face her, I sat back and crossed my legs. Stephanie stared off into the ether. When she did move, it was the same motion—reaching for the phone and then retracting her hand before touching it. I lost track of the number of times this happened before I intervened.

I walked over, removed the entire phone assembly from her desk, and placed it in my lap as I took a seat across from her. "Talk."

"I dislike that I failed to see it before. Mr. Hunt."

The implication was plain. I nodded, glad for some forward motion. Dialing took a matter of seconds, and after convincing two receptionists to forward me, I had Hunt on the line. Placing the phone on the desk, I turned on the speaker and sat back to listen.

Stephanie leaned forward, knitting her hands together. "Mr. Hunt, Stephanie Hawthorne." He replied that he recognized the voice. "Commendable. I need to speak with you. Be here at my office within the hour to discuss Miss Mary Thone."

The other end of the line was silent for a good minute before Hunt spoke again. "I don't know any Mary Thone. You must be mistaken."

Stephanie made a sound. Don't ask me to repeat or describe it. I can't. All I can say is she combined derision and doubt in one go. "Nonsense. You and I both know that for a lie. I expect you here within the hour, or I'll share what I know with the authorities."

"You can't do that!" Hunt's trademark squeak echoed through the speaker.

"Tripe, Mr. Hunt, pure and simple. I can and I will. Should I go into detail for you? I wonder what would happen should every major news outlet in the state learn of Mary Thone, the prostitution ring, and their connection to Mrs. Vice."

"That's blackmail." Again, a squeak.

"Is it, Mr. Hunt? I'm just giving you a chance to explain yourself before I am forced to report what I know to the police. As required by law." I knew that tone. Stephanie had enough to control events. Hunt had lost; he just didn't know it yet. "Mrs. Vice is welcome to join us, of course. This involves her as well. She'll want to be a part of events sooner or later. Now is as good a time as any."

"I'll be there."

The call ended, and I clicked off the speaker. Stephanie sat back in her chair and closed her eyes. I returned to my desk to await the arrival of Mr. Hunt.

Chapter 20

"In naming one a murderer, I wish it was as simple as stretching out my finger and proclaiming 'Arrest that man. He murdered X.'"

Stephanie's hand left the phone only when I sat Jeffery Hunt and Patricia Vice before her desk. Hunt's face was pale and jaundiced next to the heat Vice exuded. They were two sides of the same coin. Both had prepared for the conversation—one ready to fight tooth and nail, the other resigned to whatever may happen.

Vice opened her mouth before I could reach my desk, but Stephanie forestalled her outburst with one of her own. "Quiet, Mrs. Vice. You are here at my acquiescence. Do *not* try me."

Vice scowled. "The impertinence. I should have pushed harder to have your license revoked. All you've done is harass my people and interfere with my campaign from day one. This is the last straw. *You* will do as I say, otherwise you'll regret it. Now, who is this Mary Thone person, and why should I care?"

Stephanie raised an eyebrow. "A congresswoman—of all people—should realize power comes in many different forms, but all of it controls. You have tipped your hand in coming here, Mrs. Vice. That was a rather poor play. Had you not known who Miss Thone was, your actions would have been totally different. If I am wrong, then leave. Go do your worst, and I shall do the same. We'll see who's left standing at the end."

Her annoyance now amplified, Stephanie focused in on Hunt. The man shrank at least two sizes as he cowered in his chair. "I shall attempt to keep this brief, Mr. Hunt. I believe you already know what my interest is, so please, no evasions. It will end all the sooner if you do not force me to pull information from you like rotten teeth. I will have the information I need."

Vice hadn't taken the hint and spoke up with the anger of the self-righteous. "What are you talking about?"

Stephanie said nothing to her but directed a single word to me, short and clipped. I walked behind Vice's chair and tipped it backward until the back hit the floor. Grabbing both of her flailing arms at the wrists, I pulled Vice from the seat and across the floor to the door. Perhaps this was an indignity for a member of Congress, and a woman to boot, but stuffed shirts don't impress me much. Lessons were often needed. Vice screamed at me to stop, but I halted only when Stephanie repeated my name as I stood in the doorway.

"Mrs. Vice, are you willing to be silent, or will Daniel finish escorting you out? Mr. Hunt is vital to my enterprise. You are not."

"I'll be quiet, you bitch." At Stephanie's nod, I let go of Vice's wrists and even went so far as offering her a hand as she scrambled to her feet. She ignored it.

Stephanie waited for us to get resettled before continuing the inquisition. "How long did you know Miss Mary Thone?"

All things considered, I was surprised at the strength I heard in his voice. "Several years. All through high school and a few years after, while we dated. She disappeared about ten years ago."

"Do you know why she disappeared?"

"Not really. Both of her folks died right after our relationship ended. I think it was too much for her. She just up and left."

"When did you reunite with Miss Thone?"

"Last year at one of Representative Vice's fundraisers. I had been on board for about a month as chief of staff and . . . I hardly recognized her, but she knew me. We talked. That was it."

"Did she disclose her method of employment to you?"

"Yes." One word. Open and shut and done.

Stephanie sighed. "Mr. Hunt."

He surrendered. "There's not much to say. I didn't learn it at first. It took time. She dropped hints during that conversation. When I finally figured it out, I confronted her about it, and she warned me off. I dropped it."

"What did she do at the fundraisers?"

"Mingled with prospective clients. But then, everyone was a prospective client. Claimed you could never have a large enough product base. Product base . . . like it wasn't people she was talking about."

"I have some further questions, Mr. Hunt, but I suspect it would be best to ask them in the presence of the proper authorities. The police will be on their way. After I make a few calls, others will be joining us as well."

"Why are we involving the police? Haven't you done enough damage already?" That was Vice, rising from her seat again. "Why are we even here? Who's this Mary Thone? I've never heard of her, yet you insinuated this involves me?"

"Will you sit?" The voice was harsh, but it came from neither Stephanie nor me. Somewhere, Hunt had found his backbone. I was pleasantly surprised. He yanked Vice back into her chair. "Shut up, all right? She knows what she's talking about. If you have any hope of getting out of this with your political career intact, I suggest you do as she says."

Stephanie nodded. "You will be needed, Mr. Hunt, regardless of your wishes. Should you agree to behave, Mrs. Vice, you may join him in the conference room."

I led them across the hall and closed the door behind them. When I returned to my desk, Stephanie was already on the phone. I settled back to enjoy the show.

Stephanie set in with no preamble. "I was correct in assuming that I'd have everything by the end of the day. I intend to unmask your murderer in my office within a couple hours and hope to hand whoever it is over to your care. You know the address." A voice roared from the phone, and Stephanie held the receiver away from her ear until it subsided. "No, I won't give you the name. I have no proof as of yet. As I said, come and find out. And be sure to bring the key to Helen Black's apartment with you. I'll have need of it." She paused, waiting for acknowledgement before hanging up. Stephanie turned to me. Instructions spilled forth, quick and precise.

This was the interesting part, when I learned most of the details I'd previously missed. If I was extra lucky, I could piece together enough to do the math for myself and tag the culprit. Today wasn't one of those days. I spun to the phone and punched in Arthur Swope's number.

Swanson answered in her usual none-too-pleasant tone, informing me that Swope had already left for the day due to a call from Robert. Again, she warned me against talking to either of them. I informed her that our contact would be limited from that point on and thanked her for her time. I'm certain my false sincerity made her grind her teeth.

I reached both Swopes at the family home. It took a bit of convincing, but they agreed to be at the office by four. Of course, our client wanted to know more, but I managed to put him off. Eventually, Swope gave up, announcing his intent to arrive early for an explanation before hanging up on me. Knowing Stephanie's habits, it would do him no good.

The next call was much easier. Jennifer was out with friends when she picked up the phone, and I explained what we needed. She promised to break away and head to the office as soon as possible. I apologized for ruining her plans and promised to make it up to her later. Laughing at that, she hung up, and I moved on to other tasks.

Between two of them—I forget which—I swung into the conference room to check on our guests. Both seemed calmer than before, in retreat from their particular extremes. They accepted my offer of refreshments.

As I headed for the kitchen, I saw Jennifer walking toward me. I gave my niece a hug before handing down instructions from both Stephanie and me. The drink order came first. Once that was done, she was to find me. When Jennifer asked about Stephanie, I told her she'd disappeared upstairs. My job wasn't to keep track of errant geniuses but to do whatever needed doing. Jennifer gave me a disgusted look and went in search of her aunt. Two minutes later, she came back downstairs in a rush, her face flushed. Apparently, Stephanie had put a bee in her ear about what was important and what wasn't. Just as I expected. I smiled to myself and went about my business.

Arthur Swope arrived first, separate from his son. The logic of that was fuzzy, but I shrugged it off. I ignored his demand to see Stephanie and ushered him into the conference room. Swope paused at the door as he caught a glimpse of Vice and Hunt. Settling the matter with a curt nod, he took a seat across the table from them.

James arrived next, another officer in tow—the same one who'd brought Helen's case file to James in his office while we were there. Retrieving the key was easier than I expected, though James still put up an argument. While he ranted, I stood by with my hand out until he finished. I asked him if he was done, and he huffed and he puffed and he put the key in my hand before heading into the conference room. My brother-in-law took a seat at the far end of the table, while his companion stood before one of the room's two picture windows. I chuckled at the scene, as none of the other guests seemed too thrilled with their presence. And knowing James, he couldn't care less.

Robert was the last to arrive, ten minutes behind the others. As I met him at the door, he gave me some lame excuse about needing to shower and shave. His appearance belied that explanation. Just as his father had, Robert stopped and surveyed the assembled crowd as I ushered him into the conference room. Unlike his father, however, he had no intention of remaining. I raised my hands and barred the doorway when he attempted to make an exit. His eyes glinted, and I could almost see him considering trying to barge his way past, but he sighed and pulled out a chair midtable, as far from everyone else as possible. Arthur's eyes bore into his son from across the table, and Robert's chin dropped to his chest.

I took a moment to look over the assembled crowd. Fortunately, no one sat in Stephanie's seat. She made her grand entrance moments later, all full of grace and a bit of vengeance, the red heels I had removed from the Swope residence in her hand. She paused at the door and looked about the room. No one garnered any specific attention save for James, who received a curt nod. Everyone else got a blanket look of disgust as she took her seat at the head of the table.

"Let me state—for Detective Hawthorne's benefit—that this isn't a sanctioned police interrogation. You're all here of your own free will and are able to leave at any time. Beware, though, as leaving early may have catastrophic consequences. That being said, I assume each of you knows why you're here. Over a fortnight ago, Mr. Arthur Swope hired me to identify the murderer of his late wife, Mrs. Andrea Swope. I intend to do so today; however, I blame each and every one of you for the length of this investigation. A woman—albeit not an innocent one—would still be alive today had you not impeded my efforts. I lay her death at your feet."

Arthur Swope shot to his feet. All those years in the courtroom had served as practice for this very moment. "That's preposterous! Why should I be blamed for her death? I lifted no knife. I hired you to find my wife's killer, not point fingers."

"Sit down, sir." Stephanie's voice cut in, clear and sharp. Swope's face turned beet red, but he dropped back into his seat. "You pontificate. You requested that I perform a job, and I accepted. Now, in fulfilling that obligation, you balk at my methods. You hired a person, not a dog. I give you a choice: either you answer what questions I pose to you—if any—and I'll hand you the name of your wife's murderer, or you may leave and learn the identity when you receive my bill for services rendered. What is your decision?"

Arthur Swope remained seated, his arms crossed. Stephanie continued. "I congratulate you on a remarkably sound choice. Now, where was I? Yes. Had any of you cooperated with me or with the authorities, you'd have saved time, effort, and a life. Instead, you hampered our investigations and acted like fools. You should be ashamed of yourselves. Unless you are the murderer, that is. Then you have run a successful campaign, but it's at an end now.

"In labeling one a murderer, I wish it was as simple as stretching out my finger and proclaiming 'Arrest that man. He murdered X.' But without proof, that's nothing but folly. Doing so, I risk slander unless proof is at hand and given before witnesses. But you share this room with a murderer. That much I can promise.

"Singling out a murderer is never as simple as reading a book. Explanations rarely happen in chronological order. Facts which at first may seem irrelevant sometimes bear the greatest significance. Take these heels, for example. Aware that the police can field an army of men that I can't conceivably afford, it seemed foolhardy to cover ground they had already scoured. Instead, I searched for an angle previously overlooked.

"Mrs. Vice, what size shoe do you wear?"

The question came as an apparent surprise to Vice, though it shouldn't have. She put on a thinly veiled show of confusion. "A size seven."

"Mr. Swope," Stephanie said to the family elder, "describe your relationship with Mrs. Vice."

Swope growled. "Professional in all things."

"Indeed. That's exactly what I meant about obstructing. I doubt it, Mr. Swope. She's an attractive and powerful woman. Power attracts like moths to a flame. Mrs. Swope suspected Mrs. Vice's influence over you, hence the visit we received. Suspicions and rumor exist for a reason, Mr. Swope. Then there are these." Stephanie indicated the heels which sat on the table before her. "I know your lie for what it is. But since I require proof, I suggest we take a page from our childhood fairytales and try the shoe on for size. If the glass slipper fits . . ."

Vice blanched, but her defiant voice echoed about the room. "How do you know that shoe's mine? Even if it does fit, that's no real proof of anything."

"Shoes are interesting things, Mrs. Vice," Stephanie said. "They pick up countless particles, including DNA. Shall I hire a lab, billed to one of your largest campaign supporters, just to prove that these heels, found inside Arthur Swope's closet, are yours? Or will you admit before witnesses to what I already know—that you and Mr. Swope engaged in an extramarital affair?"

Vice's shoulders slumped as she slid down in her seat. "Blackmail. That's what this is. All right. Arthur and I spent some time together. Intimately. For the record, it didn't start that way. At first, everything was innocent. It just . . . evolved."

Stephanie nodded. "It almost always starts innocently. All the same, Andrea Swope feared your influence over her husband. That's why she wished to hire me. The act of a loving wife, fearing for the future of her marriage.

"Or was it? Such motives bear no resemblance to Andrea Swope's character. She was a petty woman, selfish and concerned with personal pleasure. That much is evident from the impressions she left behind. Wherever she went, she sowed chaos and left dissatisfaction in her wake. Over the past ten years, she spent time with countless charities, never lasting more than a few months with any. Yet, a local animal shelter kept her around for years."

"Helen's charity," Robert whispered, though the words floated through the room for all to hear.

"Indeed. Mrs. Black and Mrs. Swope shared a secret. Something tied them to that place. Whatever the secret was, I needed it in order to understand Mrs. Swope's murder. However, Mrs. Black refused to talk, causing a delay while I searched elsewhere for information.

"Fortunately, I found answers inside the room where Mrs. Swope was murdered—one of them being those heels. Another was the lack of almost all jewelry of any value. At first I wondered where the real jewelry was, but that was the wrong question. In a heist, robbers will take anything of value and easy to fence. Jewelry fits that description. And, while Mrs. Swope's jewelry was paste, the pieces were exquisitely made and not obvious copies. So why was it left behind?

"There were other clues, but perhaps the most telling was the murderer's single mistake. Let's call the murderer "Z". Z believed that without the bullet, the gun would be useless. So an attempt was made to recover it. In prying it loose, however, the bullet was lost. I imagine that, given more time, the murderer would have found the bullet and disposed of both it and the gun. But with the bullet missing, Z left the gun behind. I'll return to this.

"During a later search, Mr. Atwell found something, the existence and significance of which our killer was unaware. Beneath the dresser, he located a receipt from a local dry cleaner's. A receipt for a rather singular red dress."

"Withholding evidence, by God!" James said, sitting forward in his chair. "What dress is this? I want to see it." He tapped out each word on the table.

Stephanie's gaze shifted to her brother. "Nuts. You already have it. By all accounts, it's the same one Helen Black wore for her murderer." She grunted. "At the time, and indeed until Mrs. Black's death, I lacked anything beyond a suspicion that the dress was connected to Mrs. Swope's murder. It worked as conjecture but nothing more. However, since we are on the topic, Mrs. Vice, what was your connection with the dress?"

Patricia Vice looked around the table. "I borrowed it from Mrs. Swope during a dinner party after I spilled wine on mine."

"If you won't give me what I want, I'll pry it from you like a nail from rotting wood. Loaning a dress to someone in a moment of kindness was beyond Mrs. Swope. She had another reason. If needed, evidence can be found to prove you wore that dress at a different fundraiser. Mrs. Swope was petty and could not escape a particular trait of the female mind: the more important the function, the less likely we are to repeat our evening wear. It baffles men, but women inherently understand it.

"Aware of your affair with her husband, Mrs. Swope took revenge as she saw fit. I am sure there were other jabs and pinpricks. Other actions were more obvious, such as the constant insults to her husband at social functions. You couldn't stay away. In fact, you both responded with an increase in ardor. But that dress held other significance. It let you know she knew about your affair. Yet, she did nothing. Why?"

"I don't know," Vice whispered.

"Because Mrs. Swope was as intelligent as she was petty. Who says she wasn't doing anything? I suspect she had no intention of changing the status quo until she was prepared. Divorce was the exit strategy. Why else would she come to visit us? She was ready.

"But the importance of the dress doesn't end there. Mrs. Vice, how did you originally obtain the dress, the first time you wore it?"

Vice looked at her chief of staff. "I asked Jeffery to locate one. He brought it to me."

All eyes turned to Hunt. He turned an eerie shade of green, but his face held an unexpected look of peace. "So we come to you, Mr. Hunt," Stephanie said. "How long did you know Ms. Mary Thone?"

"Wait a second!" James was on his feet. Again. "Who's this Mary Thone, and what's she got to do with this?" Stephanie glared at her brother, who threw his hands into the air with a cry of frustration and started pacing along the back wall.

Hunt mumbled something that I missed and Stephanie chided him. "Please sit up and say that again, Mr. Hunt."

Straightening in his chair, Hunt cleared his throat before speaking. "I knew Mary back before she graduated from high school."

"And the dress?"

"I bought it for her for a formal get-together about three years after her graduation. She said she liked it—and I loved it—but she wore a different dress that night when I picked her up."

"That must have caused some tension."

"It did. We stopped seeing each other a week later."

"And when did you reacquaint yourself with Ms. Thone?"

"I told you already."

Stephanie grunted. "Must I use the same stick with you as with Mrs. Vice? Indulge me."

"At a fundraiser for Representative Vice."

Patricia Vice jerked her head at Hunt so fast, I expected her to pull a muscle. Stephanie ignored it and went on. "Did you borrow that dress from Ms. Thone?"

"Yes."

Stephanie nodded. "Satisfactory. Why did you choose to do so?"

Hunt shrugged. "I liked it. It was a classic style that's always in fashion, and I enjoyed seeing my favorite women dressed that way. Mary had no problem with me borrowing it. I was actually surprised she still had it."

"For the sake of accuracy, I request you use her correct name. At that time, when you borrowed the dress, Mary went by a different name. Tell us that name." Hunt mumbled something. "Speak up. Mumbling an answer will not save you from the indignity. I want it louder. The good detective wants to know."

Hunt threw back his head and fairly sobbed the name. "Helen. Helen Black."

"Thank you." I could tell from Stephanie's voice that she was tiring of this game. "I suspect you wanted that particular dress for a specific reason. You have feelings for Mrs. Vice. Am I correct?"

Patricia Vice looked stunned as Hunt nodded. "Jeffery . . ."

I hadn't seen it coming. I doubted anyone had besides Stephanie.

"Why are you surprised, Mrs. Vice? You're an

attractive and powerful woman. His feelings only seem natural. He wished to impress you, both as his boss and as a woman. So Mr. Hunt gave you something he cherished. Under other circumstances, it might have been romantic. Instead, you saw him only as your chief of staff. Imagine the pain as he covered for your trysts with Mr. Swope. Then came the party when Mr. Swope marked the dress—in a uniquely male fashion. How must Hunt have felt when you left the dress there, only to remember it months later? Surely the cover story you and Mr. Swope had meticulously prepared would explain everything away. However you explained its absence, it didn't work.

"The murderer knew where it was and could not stand it. It would bring nothing but ruin—something to be avoided at all costs. Perhaps if you'd stopped after that night, nothing more would have happened."

Both Vice and Swope reddened at this—she reddened from embarrassment; he reddened from anger. Stephanie continued unabated. "But, in my own way, I am thankful you didn't. I doubt secession from your entanglements would have stopped Mrs. Swope, but at least it provided me the dry cleaner's receipt. It must have slipped from your purse during one of your sessions, Mrs. Vice."

Stephanie's eyes swung to Robert. "Mr. Swope,

what was your wife's profession? There is no point in hiding it—everyone in this room knows. I ask for the record."

Robert hadn't shifted since taking a seat. His lips barely moved as he said the two words. "A prostitute."

"What was her relationship with Mrs. Swope like?"

"Rough." Robert shrugged. "But isn't that normal for most relationships between mother and daughter-in-law?"

"True. Also true for employer and employee. I suspect that, had we had the opportunity to ask, we would've found that Mrs. Black served not only as a prostitute but as a madam. To be more precise, Mrs. Andrea Swope's madam.

"That's why all the jewelry at the house was paste; the real jewels were at Mrs. Black's apartment. Both of them knew it would be much easier to remove the entanglements of marriage than those of prostitution. So the apartment became the perfect hidey-hole.

"Mrs. Swope saw the success of Mrs. Black's enterprise and wanted a piece of it herself. She knew she would never dethrone her daughter-in-law, so she set out to build her own empire. Helen's methods had worked before. This city is rife with charities which would provide the perfect cover. And the client base was there—those that Helen had ostracized or banned. Why not try for a repeat performance?"

Robert shot to his feet, the sudden movement startling half the table. He pumped his finger directly at Stephanie. "You lie!" James walked over, grabbed Robert's shoulders, and shoved him back down into his seat.

"Ask your father," Stephanie snapped. "I suspect he knows the truth of it." All eyes shifted to the elder Swope, who nodded without speaking. "That's why, despite the risks, Mrs. Black never removed Mrs. Swope from the animal shelter. To do so was to lose a valuable asset and set up a potential rival. She couldn't risk it. Mrs. Swope knew that. She knew how successful charities worked as a front. That's how she kept destroying them. None fit her needs, leaving her tied to her daughter-in-law. And that was unacceptable to her murderer. Can you imagine the scandal that would result from the revelation that a high-class lawyer, a high-end hooker, and a congresswoman were in the midst of a love triangle?"

Stephanie suddenly focused all her fury on Robert. "Do not feign ignorance, Mr. Swope. You knew such a scandal would tear your family apart. Your career, precarious at best, would be over without your father's influence. Besides, you always craved your father's approval. What better way to earn it than to stop such a catastrophe in its tracks? So you took matters into your own hands and murdered your mother."

The room stilled with those words. James, who hadn't moved from behind Robert, now placed his hand on the man's shoulder. Robert failed to notice.

At that moment, a knock on the door startled almost everyone. Stephanie feigned surprise as Jennifer entered the room.

"What is it?" Stephanie snapped.

Jennifer flushed. Right on cue. "I found this outside and thought someone here might have dropped it. I wanted to return it." She held out her hand and displayed the key I had given her earlier.

Everyone looked at it. Only Robert moved, checking his pockets before shrugging off James's hand and taking the key. "Thank you. Now I can get home."

He stuffed it into his pocket without looking at it. Stephanie waited until Jennifer slipped out and closed the door behind her. "Where was I? Yes. Who would suspect a loving son of committing such an act? And I suspect you regretted it, much like an owner regrets having to put down a faithful pet. But it was for the good of the family."

"You have no proof."

"Don't I? What makes you so sure?" Stephanie

reached into her pocket and withdrew a piece of paper. She flattened it on the table, revealing a fragment of misshapen metal. "This is the bullet that killed Mrs. Swope. I am sure tests will confirm it."

"Where did you find that?" The anger had drained from Robert's voice as quickly as the blood from his face. James looked to be supporting, rather than restraining, the man.

"Just before her death, Mrs. Swope brought home a kitten. When you pried the bullet loose, you lost it, but the cat found it. I am sure the bullet made a wonderful toy. Knocking it around the house complicated everyone's attempt to find it. However, should anyone have considered the cat, searching her favorite areas of the house might have made a difference. This was in the kitchen behind her food dish, apparently knocked out of reach. I suspected the bullet lost, but luck must eventually turn away from the villain. She's a fickle mistress.

"But the bullet is practically useless in identifying a murderer. The oils left from fingerprints are long gone, destroyed in the discharge. And while the tale Mr. Atwell circulated about etching in the metal is mostly true, the costs are still prohibitive. That story served but one purpose—to make you react. You did that admirably. You started searching, but you needed something more. A better opportunity. Mrs. Black's death provided that opportunity, allowing you to search your father's house unhindered. The distraught son returning home provided a wonderful excuse to comb through your father's house, Mr. Swope.

"But she died for other reasons. Perhaps it was to finish cleaning your family of the taint of prostitution, but I suspect there was more to it than that. She knew you killed Mrs. Swope. I am sure that for a man capable of killing the one woman who loved him unconditionally, murdering a wife was simple. Did she give you away in a moment of weakness? Could she no longer keep your secret? Evidence can be found once you know what to look for.

"Take, for example, your claim that you had no idea where Mrs. Black plied her trade. Yet that key you hold, claiming to unlock your house, in fact opens the apartment where your wife was killed."

Robert didn't deny it. Instead, he opened his mouth and in went the key. He swallowed. James wasn't fast enough to stop him. I just watched, not interested in interfering and a minor scuffle ensued.

Eventually James won. He stood up and hauled Robert to his feet. I smiled to myself, as James barked orders for everyone to accompany him to the police station. None of the other guests seemed to be in the mood to balk. The female officer led Robert out, with James playing clean-up.

James returned a minute later. "You, too, Danny Boy."

I shook my head. "Not happening. You know where to reach me if I'm needed, but you got plenty of witnesses there. One more won't make a difference."

My brother-in-law snorted. "You compromised evidence. You're coming along."

"No. But I do owe you this," I said, pulling the original key out of my pocket, still sealed in its evidence bag. "I don't need the other one back. It won't fit Mom's locks anymore."

James growled and snatched the key from my hand before stomping out. Looking about, I couldn't help but notice the room's disrepair. Jennifer was long gone, and Stephanie had skedaddled sometime during the scuffle, leaving the room empty save for me.

I started setting it to rights.

Chapter 21

End

Two days after Patricia Vice's reelection, Robert Swope was found guilty on two counts of first-degree murder. Stephanie and I only discussed it briefly before moving on to other matters. Such were our lives.

The next morning, I personally delivered our bill to Arthur Swope. Neither he nor Miss Swanson was happy to see me. That was fine, since I had no inclination to linger. It was a civil affair with little chitchat. In and out in less than three minutes. A week later, I received an envelope in the mail from the Swope Law Offices. It was empty save for a check made out to Stephanie Hawthorne; the memo line read "paid in full."

There wasn't a hold upon deposit.

The Red Dress

Nicholas Hughes

ABOUT THE AUTHOR

Nicholas Hughes lives in South Bend, Indiana.
You can follow him on his blog at
hugheswrites.wordpress.com